'What man is going to drive past a girl wearing virtually nothing. . .?'

Courtney had been taken aback by the dislike and contempt in his eyes, but now her pride was fighting back. Who did Lefteris Markakis think he was? 'I couldn't care less what you think! I don't need a man to change the wheel any more than I need a lecture from a rude, arrogant bully! I'm quite capable of dealing with my own problems.'

'You don't look like a very capable type to me. . .'

Dear Reader

Kalos orissate! That's 'You are welcome!' This month's fascinating European island is Crete, the land of *philoxenia*, or 'love of strangers'—an island famous for the warmth and hospitality of its people. Maybe your stay will be a short one—although the memories will surely last forever—or maybe, like Jessica Hart's heroine, you'll find you never want to leave! Whatever happens, 'May you always be happy!'—*Panta khara*!

The Editor

The author says:

'My first memory of Crete is of being surprised that it had taken me so long to get there. How could I have spent years trotting off to far-flung parts of the globe in search of spectacular scenery when here, right at home in Europe, was one of the most beautiful places I had ever seen? Crete had everything: breathtaking mountains and wonderful beaches, dramatic gorges and lush valleys, a vivid history and a lively present. All this *and* good food and good wine! It was, in fact, the perfect setting for romance. . .'

Jessica Hart

★ TURN TO THE BACK PAGES OF THIS BOOK FOR *WELCOME TO EUROPE*. . .OUR FASCINATING FACT-FILE ★

LOVE'S LABYRINTH

BY
JESSICA HART

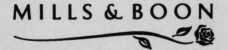

MILLS & BOON LIMITED
ETON HOUSE, 18–24 PARADISE ROAD
RICHMOND, SURREY, TW9 1SR

*First published in Great Britain 1994
by Mills & Boon Limited*

© Jessica Hart 1994

*Australian copyright 1994
Philippine copyright 1994
This edition 1994*

ISBN 0 263 78452 5

*Set in 10 on 10½ pt Linotron Times
01-9404-59493*

*Typeset in Great Britain by Centracet, Cambridge
Made and printed in Great Britain*

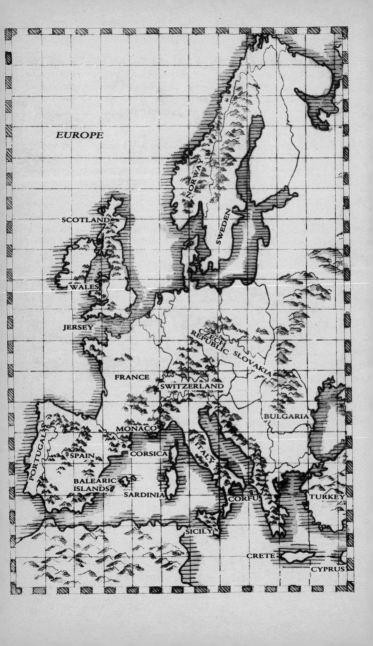

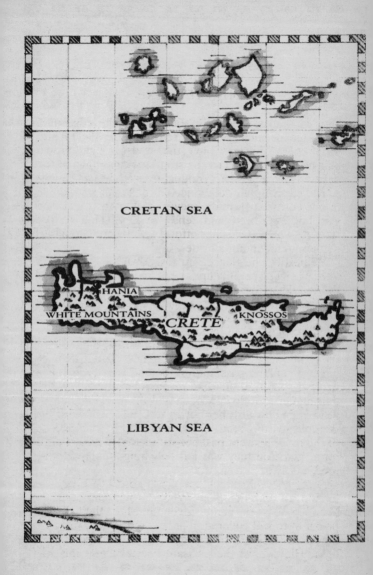

CHAPTER ONE

THE car had slewed to a standstill at the edge of a dusty road, high in the foothills of the White Mountains. Courtney blew the wisps of light brown hair off her forehead as she stood looking down at the deflated tyre in despair. A puncture was all she needed!

The car had an oddly dejected look as it sank down in one corner. Courtney knew exactly how it felt. She was hot and tired and tense from clinging to the steering-wheel as if sheer effort of will were enough to get her up the mountainside.

Helplessly, she glanced up and down the road, but it only zigzagged emptily up the hill and disappeared over the shoulder. She could hear the local bus laboriously rounding the bend below her. There was no use expecting any help *there*. The driver had taken a perverse pleasure in lumbering along ahead of her for the last forty minutes, moving out into the middle of the road whenever there was a slightest chance that she might be able to pass, and in the end it had only been sheer desperation that had given her the nerve to risk putting her foot down. Much good it had done her! It was coming towards her now, gathering speed after the tortuous hairpin bend. Churning up dust from the side of the road, it swept past her with a derisive blast of its horn, and Courtney was left coughing and spluttering in its wake.

She sighed. Rubbing the dust from her eyes, she looked around her. The White Mountains certainly lived up to their name. Even in May, their jagged peaks were still covered in snow, and below, the bare limestone crags were bleached by the fierce Cretan light. High above the pleasant coastal plain, this was wild country, a land of myth and savage passion. To Courtney, her eyes accustomed to the soft green of England, the landscape had a harsh, intractable beauty that appalled and fascinated her at the same time. The light had an intense, timeless quality, and it was easy to imagine Crete's high-booted brigands striding over these hills in search of freedom or revenge.

It was very quiet up here. Courtney could hear bees drowsing over the thyme bushes and, far above her now, the sound of that hateful bus changing gear as it rounded yet another bend in the road. She was quite alone, except for a few goats browsing on the other side of the road, their bells clanking in a desultory way as they moved between the clumps of sage and holly-oak. One of them stopped eating long enough to lift its head and stare across at her with uncomfortably intelligent eyes before it return to its nibbling, patently unimpressed.

Courtney was used to that sort of look. It was like the one her parents had given her when she had announced her intention of taking a job in Crete for the summer. In fact, she couldn't remember a time when anyone had been anything other than unimpressed. She had grown up knowing that she wasn't an impressive sort of person, certainly not when compared to her sister. Her hair was an indeterminate shade of brown, her eyes a dreamy shade somewhere between grey and blue. She had long ago accepted that she wasn't very clever, or very practical, or very attractive. She wasn't very anything. She was just Courtney.

'I'm not looking my best,' she excused herself out loud to the goat. 'I've had a hard day.' She had been travelling since six o'clock that morning, and just about everything that could go wrong *had* gone wrong. Her parents had refused to say goodbye, the taxi hadn't turned up, the train had broken down, the plane had been delayed and when she finally arrived in Heraklion she had been shown a ramshackle car and told to drive for another four hours along hair-raising roads in exactly the opposite direction to the one she wanted to go. And now a puncture!

After all that, it wasn't surprising that she looked a mess, she thought, glancing ruefully down at her sweat-shirt and shorts, both limp and irretrievably crumpled now. She had been glad of her sweatshirt on the air-conditioned plane, but it had been far too hot in the car, and she plucked at the neck in a vain attempt to cool herself down. She could feel the sweat trickling down her spine, and knew that if she looked in the mirror her face would be bright red, the wispy fringe sticking damply to her forehead. Any minute now, she would expire!

If only she had something on underneath, she could simply take it off, but she had always loathed wearing a bra, and she could hardly turn up topless to her new job. She *could* change into something cooler, though, Courtney suddenly realised. It wasn't as if there was anyone around to notice. Goats didn't count.

There was a white sleeveless vest lying near the top of her case. She took it out and laid it on the seat, ready to grab quickly if necessary. It would be just her luck if a car appeared just as she was in the middle of changing, but when she glanced up and down the road it was deserted.

The goat ignored her as she pulled her sweatshirt over her head with a sigh of relief. Typical, Courtney thought with a wry smile. She could strip off all her clothes and run around stark naked, and she would still go on being ignored! She just didn't seem to be the kind of girl people—or goats—noticed. She had a quiet, heart-shaped face with fine bones and big, dreamy eyes. Not a face that anyone ever looked twice at, unless she smiled, when people would blink and wonder why they had never noticed her before.

She tried a smile on the goat, but it didn't have any

effect. 'Be like that, then,' she said, offended, and stuck out her tongue.

The slight breeze was bliss against her bare skin, and she forgot the goat as she stood for a moment, the sweatshirt clutched to her chest, looking down the deserted valley and letting the sun glance off the smooth length of her back. It felt so good that she was reluctant to cover up again, but at last she dropped the sweatshirt and pulled on the vest. It was light and cool and comfortable, and she felt a little more capable of tackling the tyre.

Hoisting the spare wheel out of the boot, Courtney felt her spirits rise. This was what she had come to Crete to do, to prove that she could cope by herself. Her parents were convinced that she would be home in a week, but she would show them that she wasn't as hopeless as everyone thought! Changing the wheel was just the first challenge.

Fired with enthusiasm, Courtney bounced the wheel experimentally on the ground, discovered that it was as flat, if not flatter, than the one with the puncture and felt her confidence evaporate in dismay as she looked from one wheel to the other and realised that she was stuck. That was what came of being confident and enthusiastic! Tears of tiredness and frustration pricked her eyes and, unable for the moment to think of anything more useful to do, she kicked the wheel.

'Stupid, beastly, bloody car!'

'Kicking won't fix it,' said a contemptuous voice behind her, and Courtney spun round, shock catching the breath in her throat, and alarm widening her eyes.

A man was standing among the spiky maquis bushes where the hillside rose above the road. Appearing as if out of nowhere, he was a dark, dramatic figure. He carried a shotgun, cocked towards the ground, and a knife was stuck casually into his waistband. In his black shirt and trousers tucked into high boots, he was the embodiment of all the stories she had read about the famous Cretan brigands, renowned as much for their heroism as for their ferocity and passion. All that was missing was the *sariki*, the black kerchief traditionally worn by Cretan men, the knots on the fringe symbolising tears of mourning.

'Wher. . .wha. . .who are you?' Courtney stuttered, and took a hasty step backwards as he jumped lightly down on to the road beside her. He had a dark, harsh-featured face with a hawk nose and a ruthless mouth, and an aura of untamed toughness that made the hairs rise on the back of her neck. He seemed part of the wild, desolate mountains and Courtney's heart thumped nervously. She thought he looked dark and dangerous.

'My name is Lefteris Markakis,' the man said. The name meant nothing to Courtney, but there was something so arrogant about the way he spoke that she half wondered if she was supposed to recognise it.

She swallowed. Growing up in a safe, middle-class English world, she had never had to face anything remotely menacing before, and now she felt rather as if she had suddenly come face to face with a tiger. This man—Lefteris Markakis—had the same quality of coiled power, the same dangerous presence.

'What are you doing with that gun?' she asked nervously. Her heart was hammering against her ribs. Belatedly, she realised that he had spoken perfect English with only the barest trace of an accent. It should have been reassuring, she supposed, but his eyes were dark and disparaging as they looked her up and down, and she was left feeling anything but reassured. 'And how do you speak such good English?' she added, too tense to appreciate how irrelevant her question was.

Lefteris Markakis obviously did. 'I do a lot of business in English,' he said with a sort of disdainful indifference that seemed to go naturally with his arrogant expression. 'And as for my gun,' he went on, glancing down at it, 'I've been out hunting—without much success, as you can see.' A mocking gleam lit his dark brown eyes. 'There is no need to be alarmed, *despinis*. I may not care for English girls, but I don't make a habit of shooting them.'

'How did you know I was English?' Courtney demanded, ruffled by the faintly contemptuous amusement in his eyes.

Lefteris nodded his head to where the goat was standing on its hind legs to nibble the lower branches of a thorn tree. 'I heard you talking to that goat,' he said, his tone leaving her in no doubt that he had found it hard to believe that anyone could be so ridiculous.

Courtney flushed and shot an accusing look at the goat as if it were all its fault that she had been caught acting like an idiot, before she realised that if he had heard her talking to the goat he must also have seen her take off her sweatshirt. Her flush deepened. 'You shouldn't have crept up on me like that!'

'Don't worry,' said Lefteris with a sardonic look. 'I'm not interested in your body, delectable though it is. I knew you were English even before you opened your mouth. Only an English girl would strip off in full view of anyone passing and flaunt her body for the highest bidder!'

'I wasn't flaunting myself!' Courtney protested furiously, squirming inwardly at the idea of his eyes resting on her body. How dared he talk to her like that? 'I was merely changing my top because I was hot. That's hardly making a public spectacle of myself!'

'It looked like it to me. I was walking across the hillside here when I saw you pull off your top and I was presented with a tempting view of your bare back for some time. It was so perfectly done that I was sure you must have known I was there,' he said, not bothering to disguise his scorn.

'Of course I didn't!' said Courtney, scarlet with embarrassment. 'I thought I was alone. I wouldn't have taken off *anything* if I'd known there was anyone watching me.'

Lefteris Markakis was unimpressed by her vehemence. 'Then why did you stand there for so long before you put on that skimpy top?' His eyes rested on her vest for a moment before travelling with an insulting lack of concern down her slender legs. 'I don't know why you bothered. Tops like that are meant to reveal as much as they are to conceal, aren't they? Or is that why you chose it?'

Horribly aware of her body burning beneath his gaze, Courtney snatched up her sweatshirt and clutched it protectively in front of her. 'I was *hot*!' she said again, her voice shaking with anger and humiliation. 'What other reason would I have for changing?'

'You might have thought that you'd be more likely to get some assistance, perhaps,' he suggested bitingly. 'What man is going to drive past a girl wearing virtually nothing and begging for someone to fix her car? English girls don't seem to mind dressing indecently and offering up their bodies if they think they can save themselves some money. Unfortunately for you, I seem to be the only man around, and I can assure you that I'm the last person likely to fall for such obvious attractions, so you could have saved yourself the trouble.'

Courtney had been taken aback by the dislike and contempt in his eyes, but now her pride was fighting back. Who did Lefteris Markakis think he was? 'And I can assure *you*,' she retorted, 'that I couldn't care less what you think! I don't need a man to change the wheel any more than I need a lecture about my clothes from a rude, arrogant bully! I'm quite capable of dealing with my own problems.'

Her face was pale with tiredness, although her chin had come up and the blue eyes flashed defiance, but Lefteris was unimpressed as his gaze swept from the soft brown hair escaping from its plait in wild disarray to the crumpled sweatshirt still clutched to her chest, and on down slender legs to her dusty sandals.

'You don't look like a very capable type to me,' he said. 'But no doubt that appealing air of helpless innocence is carefully cultivated?'

Courtney didn't know whether to laugh or explode with fury. She was used to people telling her that she wasn't very capable, but no one had ever suggested that she might be clever enough to be doing it deliberately! 'I was about to change the wheel myself,' she pointed out coldly. 'I can't see that there would have been any point in standing around hoping that some man would come along and help me — especially not if you're an example of how friendly the people are round here!'

Lefteris looked at her with hard eyes. 'If you want to convince me that you can look after yourself, let's see you change that tyre!'

'I can't,' said Courtney, biting her lip.

'I thought not! Now that you've made your claim for independence, no doubt I'm supposed to take pity on you and offer to change the wheel for you?'

'You're welcome to try if you think you can do anything useful with two flat tyres,' she said tartly and his dark brows drew together in a frown.

'You mean you haven't got a spare?'

'I've got a flat one.' Courtney gestured to the wheel lying on the ground.

Lefteris laid his gun on the roof of the car and bent to examine the tyre. Did he think she didn't know a flat tyre when she saw one? Courtney wondered crossly. He had an air of arrogant assurance that irritated and intimidated her at the same time.

'You certainly won't get very far on that,' he said, straightening. 'It's very unwise to set out on lonely roads like these without a spare,' he added severely. 'Why didn't you check it before you left?'

Courtney eyed him with resentment, surprised he

hadn't accused her of puncturing the tyre herself just so that she could entrap some unsuspecting male into helping her! 'I've come straight from the airport at Heraklion,' she explained, conscious of how defensive she sounded. Lefteris reminded her a little of her sister, Ginny. Life didn't play nasty little tricks on them; instead they had it firmly under control. Ginny would never have been caught stripping off her clothes. She would have been wearing something cool and practical in the first place, and even if she *had* taken off her top no one would have come along to embarrass her. And she would certainly have checked her spare wheel. Courtney suppressed a sigh. 'I just assumed they would have checked the car before they gave me the keys.'

'Assumptions are dangerous things,' said Lefteris. 'Especially in Crete.'

'It doesn't seem to stop you making an awful lot of assumptions about me,' Courtney pointed out sourly. Slumping against the car, she mopped her face with the arm of the sweatshirt and blew at her fringe. She was hot and tired and fed up and wished he would just go away so that she could have a good cry in private.

'That's because I've learnt about English girls the hard way,' he said, retrieving his gun from the car. 'Where were you heading?'

'A village called Agios Giorgios,' she said a little sullenly. She would have liked to tell him to mind his own business, but there was no point in cutting off her nose to spite her face. 'Do you know it?'

'Of course.'

Of course. He probably knew everything, Courtney thought with another inward sigh. 'Is it near enough to walk?'

'No.' Lefteris studied the slender, drooping figure by the car. 'Not for you, anyway. It's over the top of the hill and at the far end of the next valley. You don't look as if you could walk as far as the next bend,' he added bluntly.

She certainly didn't feel as if she could walk anywhere. Courtney's eyes darkened to grey in dismay as
she looked down the valley to where the road snaked
into the distance, still and utterly empty. She might be
here all night if she waited for a lift.

'It looks as if I'm going to have to walk anyway,' she
said, pushing herself upright with an effort. 'I can't stay
here forever.'

'My car is parked on a track down there.' Lefteris
jerked his head down the hill as he shifted the gun
under his arm. 'You'd better come with me.'

Hardly the most gracious offer Courtney had ever
received! 'I'd rather walk,' she refused, equally rudely.
'I'd hate to think that I'd lured you into giving me a lift
after all you've had to say about English girls!'

'Oh, don't worry, I'm under no illusions about you,'
he said. 'I'm not at all susceptible to your charms, in
spite of your very inviting striptease!'

'Then why bother offering me a lift?'

'If I thought there was any alternative to leaving you
here all night, I wouldn't. As it is, I don't seem to have
much choice. I can hardly abandon you here, even if
you are English, and who knows? Another more
gullible fool might come along and give you a lift
eventually, and I wouldn't wish an entanglement with
an English girl on anyone. At least if you come with
me there's no risk of my getting involved with you.'

'Charmingly put!' said Courtney, white with anger.
'You can keep your lift, Mr Markakis. I'd rather walk
all night than accept anything from you!'

Stuffing her sweatshirt defiantly back into her suitcase, she dragged it out of the car, snatched the keys
out of the ignition, and set off up the road without a
backward glance.

Her suitcase was very heavy and the hill was steep,
but she refused to look back to see what Lefteris was
doing. He was unsufferably rude and unbearably arrogant! How dared he talk to her like that? Fury carried

her the first hundred yards, but after that she began to flag and she put her case down for a rest while she wiped her face with the back of her hand.

The road was dry and dusty, and on either side clumps of yellow-headed sage and prickly hollyoak seemed to be flourishing in the barren soil between the rocky outcrops. She could hear the bees still droning among the herbs, and there was an occasional faint clank from the goats who had moved further down the hill, but otherwise all was silent.

Risking a glance over her shoulder, Courtney saw the car looking abandoned by the roadside below her, but Lefteris had gone. He had obviously decided to leave her to it.

Well, good! The last thing she wanted was to be beholden to *him*!

Still, he might have tried a little harder to persuade her. He had seen how tired she was, and he knew even better than she did that she was unlikely to get another lift. Courtney looked up the hill in despair. Would she ever make it to Villa Athina? All she wanted now was for this day to be over. She imagined herself arriving at long last at a neat, clean little villa with a gushing shower and a soft bed. If only she could get there, everything would be all right, she told herself. Picking up her suitcase once more, she toiled on up the hill.

Puffing and panting with effort, she had stopped twice more before she heard the car behind her. She looked round eagerly, hoping that her luck had changed at last. A very smart four-wheel-drive swept round the bend below and roared up the hill towards her, but her face fell when she saw who was sitting behind the wheel.

The car stopped right beside her. 'You may as well get in,' said Lefteris, coming round to pick up her suitcase and throw it in the back next to her spare wheel. 'Pride won't be much comfort to you when it gets dark and you're still walking.'

Courtney eyed him with hostility. Look at him, taking charge of her suitcase and just *assuming* that she would fall on his neck with gratitude! On the other hand, what was the point of plodding on for hours when he could get her there in a few short minutes? Villa Athina and its comfortable bed beckoned temptingly as she hesitated, chewing her lip. As if to emphasise the point, her stomach rumbled, reminding her that she hadn't eaten since the miserly meal on the plane. Someone from Discovery Crete might have left some food at the villa for her. . .

Lefteris was holding open the passenger door with mock-courtesy, his eyes gleaming with sardonic amusement as he watched pride battling with temptation in her expression.

'Well?' he said. 'Are you coming or not?'

Temptation won. Courtney cast him a look of dislike as she climbed stiffly into the car. There was no need for him to look as if he was enjoying her humiliation quite so much!

She settled back into her seat with reluctant appreciation. She didn't know very much about cars, but this one was obviously very comfortable, very powerful and very expensive. Courtney stole a sideways look at Lefteris as he got into the driver's seat. He was dressed for the mountains, but he was obviously much more than a simple hunter. She wondered what sort of business he was in. Her only clues were that it was evidently profitable, at least to judge by this car, and he clearly didn't make his money by charm! She found her eyes resting on the implacable line of his mouth and she gave a small shiver. Whatever he did, she was sure he was utterly ruthless about it.

He started the engine and the big car pulled smoothly out on to the rough road. It powered up the hill, swinging easily round the tight bends. It was big enough to push anything out of its way, Courtney thought, remembering how she had crept around every hairpin bend in first gear, her hands slippery on the steering-wheel, too terrified to overtake the bus. Lefteris drove as if he owned the road. No doubt the bus driver would have moved smartly over for *him*!

'I'm Courtney Shelbourne,' she introduced herself awkwardly when he made no move to break the rather tense silence.

His dark eyes flickered over her. 'How very English,' he mocked. 'Tell me, are you as English as your name, Courtney Shelbourne.'

'I suppose that depends on what you think the English are like,' she said cautiously, and he gave a harsh laugh.

'My experience of English girls suggests that they're treacherous, promiscuous, immoral gold-diggers who are quite shameless about what they'll do and who they'll use to get what they want.'

'I'm not like that!' Courtney protested, taken aback by the bitterness in his voice.

'Oh? What *are* you like, then?'

Courtney shrugged helplessly and stared out of the window. She knew what her parents would say: shy, stupid, muddled, hopelessly inadequate. 'There's nothing special about me. I'm just. . .ordinary.'

She was very conscious of Lefteris beside her. He had a dark, vibrant presence that could never, ever be called ordinary. He drove with his hands relaxed on the steering-wheel, but there was no disguising the latent power in his body or the strong, striking lines of his face. His hair was black and thick and the hawk nose gave him a fierce, proud look that was emphasised by that ruthless mouth. Courtney jerked her eyes away. Just looking at it gave her a strange feeling in the pit of her stomach. She hoped it was just hunger.

'Do you really think an ordinary girl would take off her clothes in public?' he asked scathingly. 'A Greek girl certainly wouldn't, but you obviously have different standards of behaviour in England.'

Courtney gave an exasperated sigh. If only she had kept that wretched sweatshirt on and stayed hot! 'You obviously have different standards of welcoming strangers here, too,' she snapped. 'I hope everyone in Agios Giorgios isn't as friendly as you!'

'What difference will it make to you?' he retorted. 'You won't be here long enough for it to matter how friendly people are. After a few hours, you'll be like all the others, pining for bars and nightclubs and all the other attractions you seem to need to make your holiday complete. I give you a day before you turn round and head back for the coast!'

'I'm not on holiday,' said Courtney in a frosty voice. 'I've come to work in Agios Giorgios. I'll be here all summer, cooking for villa parties.'

At least she had the satisfaction of surprising him. His straight dark brows shot up. '*Villa parties*? In Agios Giorgios? It's miles off the tourist track!'

'It's being promoted as a place for people who want to get away from it all.' Courtney looked out over the empty hills and reflected that they would certainly be coming to the right place. 'The whole point is that there won't be any other tourists around. Our guests will be people who want to walk or paint or look for wild flowers without worrying about shopping or cooking in such an isolated place. That's what I'll be there for.' She hoped she sounded more confident than she felt. She could cook — that was one thing she *could* do — but she was nervous about having to act as a jolly hostess. Her parents' dinner parties always left her tongue-tied and stammering.

'It sounds very unlikely,' said Lefteris caustically. He glanced at her and then at the wild hills, and shook his head. 'I don't imagine that Agios Giorgios is quite what you had in mind when you decided to come to Crete for the summer?'

'No.' Courtney brooded, remembering her dismay as Discovery Crete's representative in Heraklion had handed her the car keys. 'You're to go to Villa Athina in Agios Giorgios,' he had said, showing her a map and pointing to the end of a long, very wiggly line leading up into the White Mountains.

'But that's over in the west!' Courtney had protested. 'They promised me at the interview that I would definitely be sent to a villa near Knossos! This Agios Giorgios is at the other end of the island!'

The rep had shrugged. 'Sorry, love. There's nothing I can do about it. All I know is that I've got instructions to send you over there. The villa is owned by one of Discovery Crete's partners, so if a guy called Nikos Papadakis turns up, make sure you're nice to him!' He had shoved all his papers back in the file and tossed Courtney the map. 'Agios Giorgios isn't actually marked on the map, but if you follow that road you can't miss it.' He had smiled with grim humour. 'It's the end of the road.'

It was also miles from all the Minoan sites that Courtney had come so far to see. She sighed. 'I thought I'd be going to a villa in eastern Crete,' she told Lefteris.

'That would make more sense,' he agreed. 'You won't find any bright lights in Agios Giorgios. The resorts on the east have far more opportunities for a girl like you.' His eyes swept disparagingly over her vest and shorts once more. 'At least you'd be dressed more appropriately there. In Agios Giorgios we prefer women to dress with a little more modesty.'

Courtney flushed and folded her arms defensively in front of her. She hoped the other inhabitants of Agios Giorgios weren't as intolerant as Lefteris Markakis. His disgust was somewhat ironic, she thought wryly. Ginny had always despaired over her old-fashioned dress sense, accusing her of being dowdy and unadventurous. It just went to show that she could never win! She glanced down at herself, wondering what Lefteris found to object to. Her top was sleeveless, it was true, but it was hardly indecent, and her shorts were made of a soft, loose cotton that came almost to her knees. They looked shorter now that she was sitting down, exposing a greater length of thigh than she would have liked, and she tugged at them surreptitiously.

They had reached the shoulder of the hill at last. Courtney didn't like to think how long it would have taken her to walk with her case. Perhaps it was worth putting up with Lefteris's snide comments for such an easy ride, she decided. Instead of leading on up the hill, as she had half expected, the road ran down into a valley, wedged, green and lush, between the barren hills and the soaring heights of the White Mountains, where the darkly dotted pines soon gave way to gaunt grey rock and snow.

Below them, the road swept around the curve of the valley. At the far end, a gorge petered out into a riverbed overhung with trees. The river divided two villages, one perched high among the pines, the other clinging to the sunny hillside, overlooking a spread of olive groves and vines and apparently ignoring the bleak hillside that loomed behind it.

'That's Agios Giorgios,' said Lefteris, an unexpected note of affection in his voice, and Courtney glanced at him sharply, wondering suddenly if there might not, after all, be a much warmer and nicer man beneath that harsh veneer. The next moment, she decided that she had been mistaken as his brows drew together once more in a suspicious frown.

'I don't know anyone in Agios Giorgios who's let a house for the summer,' he said thoughtfully. 'Are you sure you've come to the right place?'

'Of course I'm sure!' said Courtney indignantly. Did he think she had driven all this way just for the fun of it? She dug in her bag for the instructions the rep had given her. 'I've even got a map of the village. Look, it says here: Villa Athina, Agios——' She broke off with a startled cry as Lefteris stamped on the brakes and the big car practially stood on its nose. 'What's the matter?' she gasped as she was jolted back into her seat.

He didn't answer, but snatched the paper from her fingers, staring down at it unbelievingly before crushing it in his hand with a vicious exclamation in Greek. Courtney was glad she didn't understand it. The blazing anger in his eyes was clear enough and she quailed as he turned on her.

'Is this a joke?'

'A j-joke?' she stammered. 'Of course not! Why on earth should it be a joke?'

'It's certainly not a very funny one,' he said grimly. The paper had crumpled into a little ball in his hand, but he retrieved it to spread it out on the steering-wheel as he frowned down at it. 'Discovery Crete,' he read the heading in an ominously cold voice. 'Who are they?'

'It's the company I'm working for,' she said hesitantly, completely unnerved by his strange reaction. 'What is it? What's wrong?'

'Villa Athina is set right in the middle of my property, that's what's wrong!' he snarled.

She gaped at him. 'But it can't be your house! It belongs to——'

'Nikos Papadakis,' Lefteris finished for her. 'Yes, it belongs to him.' There was no inflexion at all in his voice, but something in the way he stared through the window as he said the name sent a chill down Courtney's spine. His fingers were gripping the steering-wheel so tightly that the knuckles showed white, and she edged away from the menace in his expression.

'I don't understand,' she said helplessly. 'Didn't he tell you that he was going to let the house?'

He turned in his seat to look at her with savage contempt. 'Nikos Papadakis has the best of reasons for not telling me, as you must know.'

'I don't know what you're talking about!'

'Really? Don't you think that innocent air is rather overdone? You seem to know all about Nikos owning the house and I find it hard to believe that he would pass up the chance of letting you in on his little joke. What would be the point of it otherwise? He must have known that as soon as I found out that I had an English girl planted on my doorstep—not to mention the prospect of endless parties of tourists tramping past my terrace every day—I would put a stop to the whole thing, which is just what I *am* going to do.'

'Put a stop to it?' Courtney echoed, completely baffled by now. 'What do you mean?'

'I mean that neither you nor anybody else will be spending the summer on my property.'

'But you've just admitted that the house doesn't belong to you,' she protested. 'You shouldn't have sold it if you didn't want anyone else to use it.'

'I didn't sell it. One of your compatriots was responsible for that. She was another innocent-looking English girl with a heart of pure steel, another of Nikos's little accomplices who didn't care whom she hurt so long as she got what she wanted.' Lefteris tossed the paper dismissively into her lap and put the car into gear once more. 'Well, it's not going to happen again. I'm not going to have another English girl flaunting herself in front of me all summer.'

'I wouldn't worry about that,' snapped Courtney. 'You're the last man I'd want to flaunt myself at! Otherwise, you'll just have to get used to me, I'm afraid. I'm not going to be intimidated out of a job. The villa is booked solid until October, and I intend to stay until the last guests have left.'

'I wouldn't count on it,' he said, a tight look about his mouth. 'If you think I'm going to let you and Nikos traipse through my grounds all summer, you've another think coming!'

'You won't be able to do anything about it,' she

retorted with a bravado she was far from feeling. 'I'm
here now.'

'Not for long, Courtney Shelbourne' said Lefteris
ominously as he swung the car round a hairpin bend.
'Not for long.'

CHAPTER TWO

COURTNEY glared mutinously through the window as they swept down the hill and through the olive groves. The trees were gnarled and black, the undersides of their leaves rippling silver-white in the breeze, and the grass below blurred with wild flowers, but she was blind to the beauty of the scene.

The arrogance of the man was unbelievable! Did he really expect her to turn round and meekly go home just because he didn't want her walking through his garden? And all because she was English! He had obviously had a bad experience with an English girl before now, but was that any reason to take it out on her? she thought resentfully. It had taken a lot of courage for her to come to Crete for this job, but she might have known that things wouldn't turn out as she had hoped. She had had a pleasant image of a summer in a quiet little villa with a sunny terrace and jolly, hospitable neighbours, but the dream faded rapidly as she glanced at the man sitting grim-faced beside her. Lefteris Markakis clearly had no intention of being either jolly or hospitable. Courtney sighed. It was just her luck to land herself in the middle of some vendetta!

She fully expected him to turf her out of the car when they got to Agios Giorgios, but instead he drove through the village and stopped outside a cluttered workshop. Several motorbikes in various stages of stripping stood propped in the road, and a mechanic with the regular features and curly hair of a Greek statue was tinkering with the engine of a battered van.

'I'll explain,' said Lefteris curtly, getting out of the car. 'You stay there.' He lifted the spare wheel out of the back as the mechanic came towards him, wiping his hands on an oily rag and they plunged into an animated discussion.

Ignoring his instruction, Courtney got out of the car, determined to assert her independence. She was quite capable of organising for her own spare wheel to be fixed! She pulled her phrase book out of her bag and began looking up the word for puncture, before she realised that she would only make herself look ridiculous. Lefteris was clearly explaining it all much more fluently that she ever could, even in English, and she ended up standing awkwardly to one side and trying to look assertive — and no doubt failing miserably, she added glumly to herself. It was hard to look positive and capable when your hair was falling out of its plait and you were longing for a shower.

The mechanic kept glancing at Courtney and grinning. She wished she were wearing her sweatshirt again. She was sure Lefteris was telling him all about how he had found her talking to goats and tearing off her clothes. Sticking her nose in the air, she sought refuge from her embarrassment behind an expression of intense haughtiness.

'Give Sifis your keys,' commanded Lefteris, turning to her at last. 'I've told him what's happened. He's going to fix both the tyres and he'll bring the car up to you some time tomorrow.'

'Bring the car up to me *where*?' she asked, half relieved at having the problem sorted out so easily, half resentful at the way he had taken matters so entirely out of her hands.

He looked at her as if she was an idiot. 'To Villa Athina, of course. That's where you seemed so determined to stay a few minutes ago, isn't it?'

'Well, yes, but from the way you were carrying on I thought you were prepared to bar the door against me!'

He gave an exasperated sigh. 'I certainly intend to put a stop to the idea of the house being used for visitors, but I can hardly turn you out with nowhere to go.'

'Big of you!' she snapped, and his eyes narrowed.

'The house belongs to Nikos Papadakis, so you can stay until he comes to tell you you'll have to go. I don't think that will be very long. In the meantime, I suggest you let Sifis have your keys.'

Courtney handed them over with grudging thanks. 'You're being very helpful for someone determined to get rid of me as soon as possible.'

'The sooner you have your car, the sooner you can leave,' he said bluntly and got back into the car. 'I'll be even more helpful and take you right to the villa. Now that Sifis has seen you, you'll be associated with me for as long as you stay in the village. Unfortunately, that means I can't abandon you in the middle of the village.'

'No wonder you wanted me to stay in the car!' she said sullenly. 'I suppose you're just giving me a lift to save your reputation?'

'You should be glad of it,' he said, turning the ignition key. 'It would be a long trek with a heavy case, but you can get out and walk if you really want to.'

Courtney cast him a look of dislike. If she made a fuss, she was sure he was quite capable of dumping her with her case. 'I might as well make use of you,' she said haughtily, and his lips tightened.

'I wouldn't expect anything else of an English girl.'

He stopped suddenly around the next bend as they came up behind a bent old lady, dressed entirely in black with a black kerchief covering her head. She was stumping down the road after a straggle of dusty sheep, but she turned at the sound of the car and gave a gap-toothed grin as she recognised Lefteris, who leant out of his window to speak to her.

The old lady had a seamed brown face, and her black eyes were sharp with interest as they flickered over Courtney. She talked volubly, wheezing and cackling with laughter, raising her gnarled hands or clapping them over her heart in such a dramatic gesture that Courtney wished she could understand what was being said.

Lefteris listened courteously and then, quite unexpectedly, he smiled. Courtney felt as if her senses had been given an electrifying jolt. Unprepared for the way his smile lit the dark, harsh face with warmth and charm, the breath caught in her throat, and she had to take a sharp gasp to get herself breathing again. It was only a smile, for heaven's sake! Somehow she had expected him to have a cold, ruthless smile, but it wasn't like that at all. His cheeks creased with humour, his teeth gleamed devastatingly white in his dark face. She couldn't see what his eyes were like, because he was looking at the old lady; she wondered what it would be like if he smiled like that at *her*.

Chance would be a fine thing, she reminded herself. He had made it very clear what he thought of English girls. A smile was the last thing she could expect from him. Suppressing a tiny sigh, she gazed through the window at the sheep, who had wandered off the road into the olives and were happily browsing knee-deep in flowers, and wondered who — or what — had given him such a dislike. There must be some reason why he was so prejudiced. . .

'Courtney?'

Courtney jerked her attention back to Lefteris who was looking at her in a peculiar way. 'This is Dimitra,' he said reluctantly, and she had no doubt that it hadn't been his idea to make the introduction. Dimitra beamed and nodded.

'Yiassou,' Courtney greeted her cautiously. It was one of the few Greek words she knew but it seemed to have the right effect. Dimitra seemed absolutely delighted with her fluency.

'*Yiassou*!' she beamed. Patting Lefteris's arm, she said something with a cackle and stepped back from the window with a final wave.

'What did she say?' Courtney asked curiously as they drove off.

There was a tiny pause. 'She thinks you're very pretty,' he said eventually, and Courtney's jaw dropped.

'Me? Pretty?' she asked blankly.

'Oh, very good!' he sneered. 'You must have been practising that artless look for months! Next you'll be telling me that no one has ever told you that you're pretty before!'

No one ever had. No one had ever noticed her, not next to her sister. Ginny was blonde and beautiful with perfect skin, perfect features, perfect teeth and perfect green eyes. Who would spare a glance for mousy hair and a pair of dreamy eyes when they could be staring at that?

'Some people might find your wide-eyed look attractive,' Lefteris conceded in a disparaging tone when she said nothing.

'You obviously don't,' she said, finding her tongue at last.

He glanced at her and then back at the road. 'I learnt a long time ago that the prettiest faces hide the hardest of hearts,' he said curtly.

A mile or so out of the village, he turned off the tarmac and on to a rough track which led through more olive groves then round and up towards the hills once more. The car lurched slowly over the ruts until they came to a halt by a high wall built of dry, honey-coloured stone. Courtney was puzzled until Lefteris opened a heavy wooden gate and gestured her through it.

It was like stepping into an oasis. A long, low flight of stone steps curved through hibiscus and oleander to a long terrace shaded by fresh new vines and bougain-villaea. It was hard to distinguish much of the house behind them, or through the fruit trees that stretched down from the terrace. Courtney recognised oranges and lemons, figs and almonds, pomegranates and mul-berries. The effect was lush and green, cool and quiet, an unexpected contrast to the craggy hillside rising behind.

'It's lovely!' she said, quite forgetting her antagonism as she clasped her hands together in delight and smiled. This was far, far better than the little villa she had imagined for herself. 'I had no idea it would be like this!'

A strangely arrested look had come into Lefteris's eyes at her smile, but his expression hardened again as he looked back at the house. 'I wouldn't have thought it was your kind of place. I have it on the best authority that it's unutterably boring here. It's too quiet, too isolated, too far from all the bright lights,' he said, his face twisting as he remembered.

'But it's perfect!' said Courtney, shocked that anyone could dislike such a beautiful place. 'I'm going to love it.'

'Not if I can help it,' he said flatly. 'This is my house. Athina is over there.'

He pointed through the fruit trees to an old stone house which stood at right angles to his. Compared to Lefteris's lovely house, it had an unmistakably neglected air, sad and unwelcoming, and Courtney's heart sank. Was this the bright little villa she had been dreaming about?

Lefteris was watching the disappointment on her face with dour satisfaction, and she made an effort to pull herself together. 'I'll — er — go and settle in, then,' she said, hoping that she sounded more positive than she felt.

She bent to pick up her case and set off through the trees, only to turn as Lefteris called her name. 'Courtney?'

'Yes?'

'I shouldn't bother unpacking, if I were you.'

Inside, Villa Athina smelt dank and musty, as if no one had opened a window for years, and the dim glow of

erratically placed electric bulbs only served to highlight
the gloom. Courtney explored the house in growing
dismay. The uneven stone floors were so thick with
dust that she left a trail of footsteps as she wandered
from one cheerless room to the next. The house had
been cleverly extended at the back to include five new
bedrooms and a bathroom, but they all had a forlorn,
unlived-in look, and in the end she carried her suitcase
to a small room above the living area. It had a heavy
wooden wardrobe that smelt damp, but she hung up
her clothes anyway, just to spite Lefteris, and made up
the bed with some rather mouldy-looking sheets. The
shower, with a little perseverance, produced a miserly
trickle of water and Courtney felt fresher, if not much
cleaner, when she had finished.

Afterwards, she went to sit in the depressing kitchen
and tried not to think about how hungry she was. She
had investigated the fridge and every drawer and
cupboard she could find, but no one had thought she
might welcome something to eat when she arrived. In
fact, it didn't look as if anyone had thought about her
arriving at all.

She looked at her watch. It was nearly nine o'clock.
She was exhausted, but now that she had started
thinking about food she knew that she wouldn't sleep.
It was too dark to read, too cold to sit still. She got up
and went out on to the terrace, hoping to take her
mind off her stomach, but it was even worse out there.
The lights from Lefteris's house spilled out warm and
welcoming through the orange trees, and the appetising
smell of cooking wafted tantalisingly towards her.
Courtney sniffed enviously. Lucky Lefteris, who had
someone to cook him a delicious meal tonight.

Did she dare go over and ask him for something to
eat?

Once the idea had popped into her head, it was
impossible to dislodge. Courtney told herself she would
rather starve than ask Lefteris Markakis for anything,

but her stomach kept reminding her how much better she would feel once she had eaten. Was her pride so important to her? He could hardly refuse if she asked for a piece of bread and a teaspoon of coffee, could he?

Courtney dithered, chewing her thumb, until the smell of cooking lamb became too much to bear. Her mind abruptly made up, she ran inside to change. Mindful of Lefteris's scathing comments about her unsuitable clothes, she pulled on a loose, soft green skirt that fell almost to her ankles and a demure white shirt. Dragging on a dun-coloured cardigan, she splashed water over her face and brushed out her hair until it bounced in thick, shiny waves to her shoulders. Ginny would throw up her hands in horror at her dowdy appearance, but at least Lefteris could hardly accuse her of flaunting herself now!

Squaring her shoulders, she walked back through the fruit trees. At the foot of the steps up to his terrace, she hesitated, stupidly nervous, until a rumble of hunger propelled her up the steps. The worst he could do was say no, after all.

She cleared her throat and knocked at the door. She almost lost her nerve again as she listened to the sound of footsteps, and then Lefteris opened the door. He had changed. Instead of the black brigand's costume, he wore beautifully tailored trousers and a pale shirt that made him look urbane and sophisticated without diminishing his aura of raw masculinity. Unprepared for this change of image, Courtney could only stare at him, the carefully prepared speech drying on her lips.

For a split-second surprise and something else flared in his eyes as he looked back at her, and then the more familiar expression of mocking hostility dropped back into place.

'Well, well,' he drawled. 'To what do I owe the pleasure? Or can I guess?'

'I was wondering. . .if it's not too much trouble. . .

whether you could let me have something to eat?'
Courtney said, stammering a little, and wishing that
she had decided to stay hungry after all. 'I didn't bring
anything with me, and there doesn't seem to be any
food in the house.'

'I'm not surprised. No one's been inside it for years.'
He frowned, and then stood back to gesture her inside.
'You'd better come in. You've timed it very well,' he
said with an edge of sarcasm. 'I'm about to eat myself.'

'I don't want to disturb you,' she said hastily. 'Really,
if I could just have a piece of bread, that would be
fine.'

'Don't tell me you went to all the trouble of changing
just for some bread?'

'I didn't want you to think I was trying to seduce it
out of you,' she snapped back. That surface sophistication was no more than an air; underneath he was just
as unpleasant as before.

His eyes swept over her, coldly assessing. 'You're far
more likely to have success looking as you do now, I
can assure you.'

Courtney's temper snapped. She had had enough of
Lefteris Markakis! 'It was stupid of me to come. I
thought you might be hospitable enough to let me have
something to eat, but obviously I was wrong!' Her eyes
were a stormy grey, and her face vivid with unexpected
anger as she turned to go, but he seized her wrist and
brought her up short.

His hand was very strong and warm against her skin.
For a moment they both looked down at the brown
fingers clasping her paler arm, and then he released
her slowly.

'I haven't refused you anything to eat,' he said, his
eyes still narrowed as if in surprise at her expression.
'You will share my meal.'

'I don't want to share your meal,' said Courtney, still
cross and shaken by the jolt of response at the feel of
his hand on her arm.

'Nevertheless, you will eat with me.' Lefteris walked to the end of the hall and shouted something down the corridor. A cheerful response floated back. 'Katina will lay the table for two,' he said to Courtney with the arrogant assurance that so riled her.

She hesitated, half tempted to tell him what he could do with his meal, but the thought of a good meal held her tongue. Judging by the appetising smells coming from the kitchen, it would be hot and delicious and there was no point in starving herself on a point of principle. Eating at his table didn't mean she had to *like* the man, did it?

When he opened a double door into a sitting-room, she made up her mind and walked past him with her head held high. It was a large room, divided by a dramatic stone arch, with a beamed ceiling and a floor laid with cool stone flags. The rough plaster walls were painted a soft white, toning with the long, luxurious sofas that were covered in a mass of cushions in the palest of pastels.

Determined to be unimpressed by such obvious and unexpected luxury, Courtney perched on the edge of one of the sofas and tried to find something to dislike about the room. Low wooden Turkish coffee-tables, antique chests and massive terracotta pots were effectively juxtaposed with modern paintings and several spectacular lamps, the whole effect was one of stylish elegance. The only thing she disliked in it, Courtney decided, was the man now handing her a tiny glass of colourless liquid. It looked like water, but smelt like pure alcohol, and when she took a cautious sip it burned down her throat like brandy, making her cough.

She looked down at the glass as if it had bitten her. 'It's raki,' said Lefteris, who had been watching her in speculative silence. 'It should warm you up, not that you seem to need much warming when your eyes flash like that. You look quite different when you're angry,' he went on almost thoughtfully, and then added abruptly, 'Tell me, why did you decide to stay after all?'

'I'm hungry,' said Courtney frankly, and was astonished to see a gleam of amusement light his face. He didn't actually smile, but there was a definite curl to his mouth and a deepening of the crease in his cheek, and for a moment she felt strangely breathless. She took a sip of her drink.

'That's honest, at least,' he said, but then the fleeting amusement died from his eyes. 'Or seems so. You look very demure sitting there, all clean and well-scrubbed in your soft clothes. Can you really be as honest and innocent as you seem?'

'Yes,' she said baldly, annoyed by the way her senses quivered wherever his eyes rested on her. 'I've told you, I'm just an ordinary girl. I've come out here to cook because I want to spend the summer in Crete. What could be more innocent that that?'

'If you were as innocent as you claim to be, you wouldn't have anything to do with a man like Nikos Papadakis,' he said.

Courtney ventured another sip of raki. It was certainly warming, as he had said, and made her feel much braver than she would normally. 'It sounds to me as if all he's doing is letting out his own house,' she pointed out. 'I don't see how you can object to that.'

'You've seen for yourself how close the houses are. There's no way anyone can get to Villa Athina without walking right past my terrace, and I don't intend to have my privacy invaded all summer—particularly not by hordes of English tourists.'

'Why on earth did you sell the villa if you didn't want anyone else living so close to you?'

'I didn't sell it. I gave it away to my brother.' Lefteris's eyes were suddenly very hard. 'It was his wife who sold it to Nikos before she went back to England. She was the kind of girl who enjoyed stirring up trouble. I warned Christos not to marry an English girl — I had the best of reasons to distrust them, after all — but he wouldn't listen.'

His face was bitter and Courtney was relieved when Katina, his big, smiling housekeeper, announced that dinner was ready, and beckoned them into a large dining-room, as simple and stylish as the rest of the house. Courtney sat next to Lefteris, at one end of a long refectory table, unable to decide whether she would have felt more uncomfortable marooned at the other end than in the enforced intimacy of sitting by his side.

She peeped at him under her lashes, wondering why he lived alone in all this luxury. He must be in his late thirties, she estimated, obviously rich, obviously successful. It seemed odd that he didn't have a wife. It wasn't as if he was physically repulsive. No, Courtney admitted reluctantly to herself. With that dark, fierce face and commanding presence he was dangerously attractive.

What had he meant when he said he had the best of reasons for distrusting English girls?

She told herself she couldn't care less if he wanted to lump her with every other English girl he'd ever met. He was stupidly prejudiced and unreasonable, but it wasn't her problem. At least the meal was worth surrendering her pride for, she thought as she tucked into a plate of vine leaves, stuffed with rice, raisins and pine kernels, and served with deliciously creamy yoghurt.

'How did you find Villa Athina, apart from empty of food?' asked Lefteris, maliciously observing how hungrily she ate. 'Not quite what you were expecting?'

'It'll be all right when it's cleaned,' said Courtney, lifting her chin. She was determined not to let him know how despondent she had felt as she'd explored the house.

'I wouldn't bother, if I were you.' He poured her a glass of wine. 'I meant what I said about not letting this idea of Nikos's go any further. Quite apart from anything else, it's not a suitable place. You and any unsuspecting tourists Nikos has duped into paying good money would be much better off in the east. You told me yourself that you'd rather be there. There's plenty of nightlife around Agios Nikolaos.'

Courtney laid down her fork. 'I don't want nightlife,' she said. 'The only reason I wanted to be in the east is to be nearer the Minoan sites.'

'Minoan sites?' Lefteris stopped in the act of lifting his glass to his lips and his dark brows shot up.

'I want to be an archaeologist,' she confessed.

To her chagrin, his mouth twitched. 'How very unlikely!' He studied her as if for the first time, surprise and an unfamiliar glint of interest in his expression. The shine of her hair reflected the light as it fell softly around her face and her eyes were a peculiarly intense shade somewhere between blue and grey as they stared back at him with more than a hint of challenge. 'I wouldn't have taken you for an academic type.'

'I'm not, really,' Courtney admitted. 'I've always wanted to study the Minoans, ever since I first read all those legends about Theseus and the Minotaur and the labyrinth at Knossos.' She leant forward, unaware of how enthusiasm lit her face to quiet beauty. 'That's why I've come to Crete. I've applied to do a course that specialises in Minoan civilisation, but I don't have any of the right qualifications. I've always been hopeless at exams, but I'm hoping that if I can study as much as I can while I'm here, and maybe get some experience on a dig later on, I might at least get an interview. I was told it was worth a try anyway.'

'All the more reason for you to go over to the east,' Lefteris pointed out. His eyes had held the same sudden arrested look as before, and now he looked as if he was struggling with unwelcome thoughts beneath a veneer of cool indifference. 'That's where all the great Minoan sites are. You'd be far more likely to impress your interviewers if you've spent your time there, rather than tied to a kitchen miles away in western Crete.'

'I know.' Courtney sat back, the light draining from her face as she remembered her disappointment when she had found out just how far away she was going to be. 'At the interview they promised me faithfully that I'd be sent to a villa near Knossos. The idea was that I could get all the shopping and preparation done in the mornings and have the afternoons free to explore the sites. I thought if I hung around enough I might be able to make some contacts so that I could join a proper dig when the Discovery Crete job was over. As it was, they sent me *here*. I know that it's very beautiful, but the White Mountains aren't exactly overflowing with Minoan ruins!'

'You should be grateful to me, then,' he said.

She stared at him. 'Grateful! How do you work that one out?'

'When no guests appear, you'll be free to go and explore Minoan ruins to your heart's content.'

'I can't afford to do that,' said Courtney, twisting the glass between her hands. 'I need this job. I'd been saving up to come to Crete on my own, but I didn't have very much put by when I got the chance to work for Discovery Crete. It all seemed so perfect.' When she had seen the advertisement in the paper, it had seemed the answer to her prayers. 'They gave me my ticket out here, and I'll be paid every two weeks. At least in a place like Agios Giorgios there won't be much to spend my money on, so I should be able to save enough to stay on for a while when the season's over. They promised they'd give me an open-dated ticket back to London.'

'But until they do you've got no money and no ticket home, is that right?'

Courtney flushed at his tone. He sounded exactly

like her father, irritated and incredulous that anyone
could be quite so trusting. 'I've got a little money.'

'Enough for a ticket home?'

'I won't need a ticket home,' she snapped, taking a
defiant gulp of her wine. She wasn't about to tell
Lefteris Markakis just how little money she had. She
had enough to stock up with provisions before the first
group arrived and that was about all. But Discovery
Crete had assured her that the rep bringing the group
to the villa would provide her with a float, and pay her
for the first two weeks. 'And I'll have plenty of money
once I've been paid.'

The second course had turned out to be chunks of
lamb cooked in a delicate artichoke sauce. Courtney
concentrated on her food and on not thinking about
how little she knew about Discovery Crete. She had
been so desperate to get to Crete before she lost her
nerve and gave in to her parents' far more sensible
suggestions that she supposed she had just grabbed at
the first job that came along.

Lefteris was silent too, as if he was reluctantly
reshuffling some of his ideas, but when Katina brought
in two cups of Greek coffee he pushed back his chair
and got to his feet. 'We'll have coffee on the terrace so
Katina can clear up in here.'

Courtney stood up too, and smiled at Katina. '*Efhar-
isto*,' she said, proudly producing one of her few
carefully learnt Greek words. 'Thank you, that was
wonderful!' She patted her stomach appreciatively to
mime satisfaction and Katina beamed back at her,
delighted.

Turning back to Lefteris, Courtney caught him
watching her with a strange, almost puzzled expression
in his eyes, but the next moment it had flickered and
gone. Shrugging, she following him out on to the
terrace. She had always enjoyed her food and she felt
immeasurably better now that she had eaten. Her
confidence rose with her spirits. It had definitely been

worth putting up with his hostility for a meal like that. All she had to do now was drink her coffee and leave, and hopefully she would be able to avoid him for the rest of the summer. Once he saw how quiet and unobtrusive she was, he would just have to accept the situation.

It was cool outside, but the night was clear and still, and the moon shone a bright silver sliver in the blue-black sky. Courtney sat on a carved wooden bench and listened to the persistent *kook kook* of the Scops owl calling through the darkness. In spite of all her renewed confidence, she was conscious of the tension trickling back into the atmosphere.

Lefteris lounged beside her on the bench, holding the absurdly small coffee-cup in his strong brown hands. Watching them, Courtney felt her arm throb where he had held her. She tried to concentrate on her own cup, but her eyes kept skittering to his profile, to the thrust of his jaw, to the crease in his cheek and the firm curve of his mouth. It was odd how familiar he looked already.

If she closed her eyes, she was sure that she could visualise him very clearly, and yet what did she know about him? Only that he confused her. She couldn't fit the tough mountain man who had appeared so suddenly on the hillside with the sophisticated businessman at home in these luxurious surroundings. There was a harshness about him, a fierce pride and an arrogant confidence that nettled her but when she remembered his smile, or the reluctant amusement that had sprung once or twice to his eyes, she found herself wishing she could know him better.

Without warning, he turned his head and caught her studying him. Courtney was glad of the darkness that hid her blush, and looked quickly away. 'You look puzzled,' he said. She could hear the undercurrent of mockery in his voice.

'I was just wondering about you,' she said candidly before she could stop herself. 'What do you do?'

'Don't you mean, how much are you worth?' he asked harshly. 'I'd have thought you'd have done a bit more research before you came out! Or has all this interest just come on since you've seen inside my house?'

'It just wasn't quite what I expected, that's all,' she said, hackles rising at his tone.

'I'm a businessman, since you're so keen to know. I own a company—several companies in fact.'

'What sort of companies?' she asked, suspecting that his offhand tone was deliberately evasive.

He raised a sardonic eyebrow. 'Largely financial, but I have subsidiary interests in communications, property development and travel. . .and shipping, of course.'

Courtney looked determinedly unimpressed. Shipping, of course! Only a tycoon could sound so casual about it! He probably *had* expected her to recognise him name.

'Wishing now that you had tried a little harder to be nice to me?' he mocked, misreading her expression. 'You started off very promisingly this evening when you came to the door all wide-eyed and appealing. I thought then that you must have known who I was, but you rather spoilt things by losing your temper, didn't you? You'll need to be a lot nicer than that if you want to get close to my cheque-book!'

'I'm not interested in you or your money,' said Courtney, white with anger. She balanced her coffee-cup carefully on the edge of the bench and stood up. 'I'm grateful for dinner, but I don't see why I should waste any time being nice to someone who has been unfriendly, unpleasant, and ridiculously prejudiced! You may have met one or two English girls you didn't like, but it doesn't mean we're all like that.'

'Doesn't it?' He had risen to his feet with her, and

was standing unnervingly close. 'Don't tell me you're going to try and change my ideas about the English?'

Courtney tucked her hair behind her ears in an unconsciously nervous gesture. 'I just think it's unfair for you to judge me, and all the guests who'll be coming to stay in Villa Athina, just because you feel bitter about someone who happens to come from the same country.'

'I prefer to base my opinions on what I know for myself,' he said. 'So far I've seen you strip shamelessly in public and wangle a free dinner by dressing up nicely. I haven't seen anything of the nice girl you claim to be. How are you going to persuade me that that's just what you are?'

'Perhaps after I've been here for a whole summer you'll be able to see that for yourself,' said Courtney bravely. His closeness was making her heart thud painfully against her ribs, and she took a step backwards, only to find herself caught by the wrist as before and pulled inexorably back towards him.

'Perhaps it won't take that long,' he countered, tilting her face up to his. Her eyes gleamed wide and frantic in the moonlight as she stared helplessly up at him, but his expression was unreadable, and then, abruptly, his mouth came down on hers.

CHAPTER THREE

THE ground dropped from beneath Courtney's feet, plunging her into sheer sensation and parting her lips in an involuntary gasp of surprise. Unthinkingly, her fingers curled into the cool cotton of his shirt as if it was her only anchor to reality. How could she ever have thought of his mouth as inflexible? It was warm and persuasive, a focus of electrifying excitement.

Beyond struggling, beyond thinking, she clutched at him, terrified by the surge of response that threatened to suck her down into a deep, dangerous well of feeling, enthralled and intoxicated by a dizzying awareness of his mouth on hers, the hard hands sliding up her arms to cup her face. His body was massive, overwhelmingly solid, and she leant instinctively into its secure strength. Her senses burned at his touch. She wanted to break away, but a treacherous desire was swirling through her veins, urging her closer, demanding more.

With a muttered exclamation, Lefteris lifted his head, and they stared at each other, both breathing heavily. 'A good try, Courtney,' he said at last. 'But I think it will take more than one kiss to convince me that you're not just like all the rest!'

Dazed, uncomprehending, she looked blankly up at him with wide, dark eyes, until, abruptly, realisation dawned. He had kissed her to prove some cheap point and she, *she* had clung to him like some lovesick idiot! A wave of humiliation hit her with the force of a blow and the colour surged up her face. She hardly knew the man, and what she did know she didn't like. How could she have let him kiss her like that? How could she have kissed him back? How *could* she?

She stepped back as if she had been stung, pressing

her hands to her hot cheeks. 'I — I think I'd better go,' she stammered.

'I think you better had,' he said.

He thought it was funny, she realised. She could hear the mockery in his voice, see the hateful curl of his mouth. It amused him that her fragile veneer of confidence had dissolved at the merest touch of his mouth, that she had melted into his arms and into his kisses without so much as a struggle.

Courtney hated him then. She opened her mouth to shout at him, to explain that she had been taken unawares, that she would never, ever have kissed him like that if she had had time to think about what was happening, but no words came out. Closing her mouth again, she took another uncertain step backwards, and then, as if suddenly galvanised into action, turned and fled down the steps and back through the trees to the safety of Villa Athina.

Courtney dragged the last mattress out on to the terrace and laid it with the others to air. In the bright light of day, the rooms looked even dirtier and more neglected than they had seemed last night, but at least the prospect of cleaning gave her something to take her mind off Lefteris Markakis. She burned with humiliation every time she remembered how he had kissed her, how she had kissed him. Why had he done it? To prove how little an English girl could affect him, or simply to humiliate her into leaving? If so, he had miscalculated. Nothing could have been more calculated to fire her resolve to stay, if only to prove in her turn how little it had meant to *her*!

Throwing open the shutters in every room, she was determined to turn Villa Athina into such a wonderful place to stay that its English guests would want to come back year after year to annoy Lefteris. She found a broom and swept the worst of the dust from the floors and the terrace before struggling outside with the damp mattresses. They were awkward and heavy, and she was red-faced with effort by the time she had finished. She stood wiping her forehead with the back of her arm and admiring the view while she got her breath back.

The sky was a deep hyacinth-blue, and the light so intense that she could almost hold it in her hands. The White Mountains rose, shimmering in the sunlight, on her right, and a gentle breeze riffled through the orange trees, swirling drifts of their sweet, almost cloying scent through the bright air.

There was no sign of Lefteris. Courtney had been annoyed to find that every time she carried a mattress out on to the terrace she had glanced over to his house. He had been insufferably rude last night; if she never saw him again, it would be much too soon!

She was about to turn away when she caught a movement through the trees, and her heart leapt, but it wasn't him. It was a stranger, dark and olive-skinned like Lefteris, but there the resemblance ended. Where Lefteris was rugged, this man was smooth. He was very handsome, although his features lacked the impact of Lefteris's fierce, dramatic face, and he was immaculately dressed in a short-sleeved shirt and pale trousers. Even his sunglasses matched.

He took them off as he strolled through the trees and climbed the steps towards her. 'You must be Courtney,' he said with a pleasant smile, and held out his hand. 'Welcome to Discovery Crete. I'm Nikos Papadakis.'

Hastily, Courtney wiped her dusty fingers on her jeans and shook his hand, trying to conceal her surprise. What could there possibly be about this attractive man to arouse Lefteris to such hatred? It just went to prove how unreasonable he was, she thought darkly, and smiled warmly back at Nikos, rather wishing Lefteris would appear to see just how charming she could be when she tried. Besides, Nikos was effectively her boss. The rep at Heraklion airport had specificially told her to be nice to him.

'I'm afraid I wasn't expecting any visitors yet,' she said, gesturing ruefully down at her grubby T-shirt and jeans.

'It looks as if you're hard at work already,' Nikos said admiringly. 'I'm afraid the house wasn't quite ready to receive visitors, which is why we asked you to come out a little earlier.'

'I've got ten days before the first group arrive,' Courtney said. 'That ought to give me plenty of time to get everything ready.'

'Excellent. Discovery Crete is obviously very lucky to have you.'

He stayed about twenty minutes. Courtney wondered if he would explain why Lefteris was so hostile to the idea of the house being used, but he didn't mention it, and after a while she began to wonder if the whole business might be a figment of Lefteris's imagination. Certainly Nikos gave no sign that there was anything untoward about the arrangement.

She walked back with him to where his car, a gleaming red, open-topped Mercedes, was parked outside the gate. She had been recalculating her finances. If she was to buy all the cleaning materials that were needed, she would soon find herself out of pocket, and she wondered if she could ask tactfully for an advance. She was still deciding how to phrase her request when Lefteris's big four-wheel-drive swung round the bend and something indefinable in the atmosphere changed.

It was the first time Courtney had seen him since he had kissed her in the moonlight, and her heart was thumping so loudly that she half expected Nikos to turn and stare at her in astonishment. She desperately wanted to appear cool and casual, but was very conscious of her grubby clothes, untidy hair and the absurdly guilty way she was standing next to Nikos.

Lefteris was quite cool enough for both of them. His

face looked as if it had been carved out of granite, and his eyes were cold and implacable as they moved from her to Nikos. Courtney could feel the hostility running tense and raw very close to the surface, and glanced at Nikos. His eyes were gleaming with such malice that she was taken aback.

'What do you think of my scheme?' he asked Lefteris with what Courtney suspected was deliberate provocation. He laid an arm over her shoulders in a casually intimate gesture. 'A beautiful old house in the heart of the Cretan mountains, with a pretty English girl to cook the comforts of home. The tourists should come flocking! I don't see how it can fail, especially not with Courtney as such a charming hostess.'

Lefteris's expression was so contemptuous that Courtney, who had decided to move away from Nikos's arm, promptly snuggled closer to Nikos and simpered up at him. Let Lefteris see how little she cared what he thought!

'Any scheme can fail,' he said, and his voice was as hard and cold as the mountains. 'You of all people ought to know that.'

A muscle jumped in Nikos's throat. 'My schemes have only ever failed because of you. You pull the financial strings round here and everyone jumps! Well, it's not going to happen this time. Villa Athina is mine now, and not even you can do anything about it.'

'Don't count on it,' said Lefteris. 'You may have persuaded Linda to sell you the house, but you don't own the ground around it, and you never will.' His eyes flicked to Courtney, still standing close to Nikos. 'Now get off my property.'

He said it without raising his voice, but the air was suddenly chill with menace. Courtney swallowed, and stepped away from Nikos, who looked from her to Lefteris and then back again, eyes narrowed.

Turning, he took her hand ostentatiously. 'Somehow I get the feeling I'm not welcome here,' he said with a brave attempt at insouciance. 'You're doing a marvellous job already, Courtney! If you have any problems — ' he glanced significantly at Lefteris ' — any at all, come and see me.' He pulled a business card out of his shirt pocket. 'Here's my address. Come and see me anyway. You don't have to have a problem. It will always be a pleasure to see you.'

Aware of Lefteris's cold eyes upon her, Courtney gave Nikos a brilliant smile. 'I'd like that,' she said with unnecessary warmth. 'I can't tell you how much better I feel knowing that I've got a friend here,' she added for Lefteris's benefit. 'I'll come and see you very soon.'

He watched grimly as she made a great show of waving Nikos off, but as soon as the red Mercedes had disappeared round the bend her nerve began to fail her. Pretending a bravado she was far from feeling, she walked towards the gate with her head held high.

'I thought you didn't know Nikos?'

'I didn't. I do now.' Courtney risked a glance as she passed him. He looked very hard, very grim and very, very formidable, the stern lines of his face set in intimidating lines. 'I don't know why you're so suspicious of him. I thought he was very nice.'

Lefteris gave a brief, humourless laugh. '*Very nice*,' he mimicked her savagely. 'There's nothing *nice* about Nikos Papadakis, believe me.'

'"I prefer to base my opinions on what I know for myself,"' Courtney quoted back his words from last night with a challenging look in her eyes. Their blue-grey deepened in intensity according to the colour of the sky. In winter they took on a grey hue, but now, with the vibrant Greek sky reflected in them, they were blue and bright with defiance.

'It didn't take you long to fall for Nikos, did it?' he said harshly. 'There must be something about him that appeals to English girls. Perhaps you recognise a

kindred spirit in him, a rotten core beneath a pretty
exterior?'

'At least he hasn't threatened me with losing my
job,' said Courtney, nerves sharpening her voice.

'I'm going to do more than threaten,' Lefteris promised grimly, and walked on up the steps, leaving
Courtney staring angrily after him.

Courtney smoothed down the last blanket and stood
back to admire the room. She had worked hard over
the last week, and now the house was ready to receive
its first guests. Every room had been swept and dusted
and polished, the bedding had been aired until it was
fresh and sweet with sunshine, and the terrace had
been weeded and brightened with some geraniums that
Dimitra had given her.

Every day, Courtney walked down the rutted track
and along the road to Agios Giorgios, and every day
she would meet Dimitra, moving her cosseted goat to
a fresh piece of grass outside her house. Dimitra clearly
remembered seeing Courtney with Lefteris, for she
always beckoned her in, beaming with pleasure.
Courtney would sit in the dim little room, looking out
through the door to a sunny courtyard where the fat
hens scratched and burbled, and Dimitra would bring
her a glass of water with some coffee and a saucer of
sweet biscuits. Then she would sit on the bed with a
sigh, rub her knees and tell Courtney about her arthritis, or produce much handled photographs of her
grandchildren. Courtney's Greek was limited to a few
phrases, but somehow they seemed to understand each
other, and every day she would increase her vocabulary
or improve her pronunciation. When she left, Dimitra
would insist on giving her something to take with her —
a couple of eggs, or a dish of creamy yoghurt, or
cuttings from the geraniums which Courtney had
planted out in some rusty olive oil cans.

She liked her daily trips to the village. There was a

butcher, a small bakery where the loaves were piled in baskets still warm from the oven, and a dark, cavernous shop crowded with sacks of flour, washing powder, tubs of margarine and great cans of feta cheese swimming in milk. Outside, a canary sang in a cage over the door, and a small, erratic selection of vegetables were stacked in wooden crates.

In the centre of the village was a *kafenion*, where the old men sat under a huge, spreading plane tree and played endless games of backgammon. Some would sit facing the street, straight-backed and stern, a cup of coffee and a glass of water on the table beside them, fingering their worry beads or holding knobbly sticks of ash between their knees. Courtney was intimidated by their harsh old faces, until she greeted them nervously, at which they all broke into miraculously charming smiles.

'*Yiassou!*' they called back, and Petros, shuffling between them, balancing a tiny coffee-cup and a wet glass on a minute tin tray, would wipe the tables and raise his rag to greet her as well.

Nothing ever happened in Agios Giorgios. Courtney thought that was probably why she liked it so much. Dogs lay panting in the shade, and chickens scratched in the road, undisturbed by anything more than an occasional young man on a Vespa. Once she saw the bus, and another time there was a pick-up truck parked in the square, its back piled high with artichokes, but that appeared to be the day's entertainment.

Sometimes Courtney would forget that she had ever wanted to be exploring Minoan ruins in the east. She would walk slowly back to the villa, her arms full of sweet-smelling bread. The track was dry and dusty beneath her sandals, and great, fat bumble bees lumbered among the poppies, so heavy that when they settled on a petal the flowers would keel gracefully over under their weight. There were drifts of tall daisies, mingling with the mauve of wild geraniums,

the soft blurry blue scabious and the froth of Queen
Anne's lace, all flourishing on the stony ground
between the silvery-grey clumps of false dittany, pungent oregano and asparagus growing wild, prosaic
dandelions and thistles and the bright yellow heads of
giant fennel, towering above the rest.

As the days had passed and she heard nothing more
from either Lefteris or Nikos, Courtney had begun to
relax. Lefteris had been angry at the thought of visitors
staying so close to his house, but his threats had been
no more than that. What could he do, after all?
Courtney's only concern was that she was running short
of money. Lefteris had interrupted them before she
had had a chance to ask Nikos for an advance, and the
cleaning materials had cost more than she had
expected.

Lefteris himself had shown no further interest in her.
Every time Courtney went outside and caught herself
glancing over towards his terrace, she told herself she
was glad. Too often, she would find herself remembering how he had kissed her, and a treacherous warmth
would uncurl deep inside her and tingle slowly along
her veins until she sternly repressed the feeling.

Once when she was taking a break from cleaning on
the terrace she had glimpsed him through the trees,
striding towards the gate in a severe suit and tie, but
he didn't so much as glance in her direction, and she
had marched back into the kitchen to relieve her
feelings by scrubbing the wooden table, without paus-
ing to wonder why she was so cross. Another time, she
saw a stream of smart men and elegantly dressed
women climbing up the steps to the terrace and the
sound of laughter spilling out over the orange trees had
gone on long into the night. She had tossed and turned
in bed, pulling the pillow over her head and then
chucking it aside, hating the way she could imagine
him so vividly. He would be moving among his guests,
negotiating multi-million-pound deals in huddles with

the men and smiling at all the beautiful women the way
he had never smiled at her.

Now, everything was ready. Courtney gave the
blanket a final twitch and went down to the kitchen
where her shopping list lay on the table. She had
planned her menus in great detail, and now all that
remained to do was to buy all the ingredients. Unfortunately, that meant a trip into the market in Hania.

Courtney quailed at the thought of the drive. Sifis
had brought the car back, complete with tyres, but
when she had taken it out for a drive it had jerked
along so reluctantly that she had turned round and
coaxed it back to the villa, where it had remained ever
since. She would have to talk to Nikos about getting it
checked, but in the meantime there was the long,
twisting, hair-raising road to Hania to negotiate.

Picking up the car keys, she weighed them in her
hand and took a deep breath. She might as well get it
over with. She seized her bag and the list, and headed
purposefully for the gate before she had a chance to
put it off any longer.

Lefteris was standing at the bottom of the steps.
Intent on checking her list in case she had forgotten
anything, Courtney didn't notice him until she was
right in front of him, and the sight of him stopped her
dead in her tracks, driving the breath painfully from
her lungs. She had forgotten the sheer impact of his
presence.

His brows rose at her expression, and she swallowed.
'I didn't see you,' she explained weakly, hoping that he
would think it was surprise that made her voice so high
and thin.

'Off to see your very nice friend Nikos?' he jeered,
glancing at the keys she was clutching in her hand.

'I'm going into Hania to stock up at the market.'
Courtney cleared her throat and tried to get her
breathing under control. He might as well accept that

everything was going to go ahead as planned. 'The first group arrive the day after tomorrow.'

'You can save yourself the trip,' he said. 'They won't be coming.'

Courtney stared at him. 'What are you talking about?'

'Discovery Crete has gone bankrupt. Haven't they been in touch with you yet?'

'I don't believe you,' she said in an uncertain voice. 'I would have heard.'

He shrugged with infuriating indifference. 'Why don't you go and ask Nikos? You seem to believe everything he tells you.'

'I don't need to ask him,' she flared. 'You're lying! You're just trying to make me leave before the guests arrive so that the company won't have any choice but to take them somewhere else.' She glared at him, her face vivid with anger. 'You needn't think I'm going to fall for a scare tactic like that!'

'I'm not trying to scare you,' he said. 'I'm just suggesting that you don't waste your money stocking up on a lot of food you're not going to need.'

'You know what you can do with your advice!' Courtney said rudely. 'I don't believe a word of it.'

'Have it your own way,' he said, unperturbed by her fury. 'But don't blame me if you end up with a lot of left-overs.'

Courtney cast him a look of loathing and banged out of the gate. She wasn't such a fool that she would belive anything *he* said! To her rage, he came out to watch her get into the car. Under his sardonic eye, she fumbled with the unfamiliar gears and stalled. Blaming it entirely on him, she muttered venomously under her breath, and finally found the right gear, only to lurch awkwardly down the track as the engine warmed up.

Rehearsing all the arguments why she shouldn't even bother checking with Nikos, she drove through the village and across the valley. At the foot of the hills, there was a turn-off that led up to the village where Nikos lived, perched high above the river. She slowed as she reached the turning. *Should* she ask Nikos if there was any truth in what Lefteris had said?

No, she wouldn't give him the satisfaction of guessing that she had so much as hesitated. Putting down her foot, she sailed past the turn-off, only to stop in the middle of the road a few seconds later. She sat, biting her lip and drumming her fingers on the steering-wheel, before she came to a sudden decision. Reversing carefully back to the signpost, she turned up towards the village.

At the tiny *kafenion*, they directed her to a big house on the outskirts of the village, where the road petered out. The house was huge and resembled nothing so much as a stranded liner, with a vast terrace overlooking the valley. Courtney heard Nikos's voice as soon as she stepped into the house. He sounded very angry about something, and when she was shown into the living-room where he banged down the telephone she hesitated, hardly recognising the pleasant man she remembered in the malevolent eyes and the face dark and twisted with fury.

He obviously wasn't expecting her, but made a heroic effort to bring himself under control as soon as he caught sight of her dithering in the doorway. 'Courtney,' he greeted her with a smile that didn't quite reach his eyes. 'What a pleasant surprise!'

'I've come at a bad time,' she said awkwardly. 'It's just. . .well, Lefteris told me that Discovery Crete had gone bankrupt. I didn't believe him, of course, but then I thought I'd better come and see you. . .' She trailed off as she saw Nikos's expression. 'It's not true?'

'It's true all right,' he said. 'I've just heard myself.'

Courtney sat down abruptly on a chair. 'But. . .what happened?' she whispered, appalled at having her worst fears confirmed.

'Lefteris Markakis can tell you that better than I can,'

said Nikos, with a vindictive look out of the window towards Agios Giorgios. 'He should know, after all.'

'What do you mean?' she asked slowly.

Nikos swung round. 'It was Lefteris who pulled the finance out of Discovery Crete.'

'But that's impossible!' Courtney was struggling to grasp the fact that there would be no guests arriving, no job, no summer in Crete. 'He couldn't have had any money invested in the company. He'd never even heard of it until I arrived.'

'Lefteris Markakis can do what he likes,' said Nikos bitterly. 'He's a much more powerful man than you realise. Do you know how many companies he owns? You don't get to be as rich as he is without being utterly ruthless about getting what you want. As soon as he knew the name of the company, all he had to do was pick up a phone, speak to a few contacts in the financial world who all want to keep on the right side of him, and bang goes one small company!'

'But *why*?' she cried. 'Oh, I know he didn't like the idea of tourists walking through his garden, but we could have worked something out. We wouldn't have bothered him. He didn't need to bankrupt the whole company!'

'You don't understand him at all, do you?' Nikos said with a bleak laugh. 'That sophisticated image is just a veneer. Underneath he's still a bandit, just like his family have always been. You mustn't ever forget that he's a Cretan, and he's got a Cretan's long memory for slights. Our families have hated each other for generations. Bankrupting a company I've invested in is just another step in his personal vendetta against me, that's all. The fact that I owned Villa Athina was enough for him to be determined to ensure that no one ever lived there. The whole idea of Discovery Crete was mine. I set it up with English partners, and as soon as he found that out the company was doomed. He's done it before. This is the third company of mine that he's ruined.'

Courtney felt sick. 'Why does he hate you so much?'

'Why? What reason does a man like Lefteris Markakis need? He cannot bear to be challenged, or to lose face.'

'So you think that he went to the trouble of bankrupting Discovery Crete and putting all its employees out of a job just to score a point off you?' The numb sense of shock was giving way to a slow burn of fury, and her hands were clenched so tightly that the car keys dug into her palm.

'I don't think, I *know*,' said Nikos. 'People mean nothing to Lefteris Markakis. He's a businessman through and through.' Courtney stared at him for a moment, then got to her feet and headed for the door. 'Where are you going?'

'I'm going to tell him exactly what I think of him!'

'Do you think that's wise? He can be a dangerous man to cross, as I know to my cost.'

'I don't care if it's wise or not,' she said through her teeth. 'I'm going.'

Nikos looked at her speculatively. 'If you're set on it, I'd better give you a lift,' he said at last, picking some keys up off the table.

'It's all right. I've got the car.'

He spread his hands in apology. 'I'm afraid I'll have to keep it here for now. I'm sure you understand. Now that our bankers have withdrawn support, we have so few assets. . .'

'Of course,' said Courtney, biting her lip. 'I'm sorry. I was forgetting that you've lost far more out of this than I have.' It was obviously not the moment to mention the money she had spent on cleaning the villa, either.

It was all Lefteris's fault. Her jaw worked with fury all the way back to Agios Giorgios as she stored up everything she would say to him. Nikos dropped her at the end of the track, and she barely said goodbye, too angry for courtesies.

Everything was quiet and peaceful as she stalked up the steps and into the house without knocking. In the cool, stone-flagged hall, she hesitated for a moment while her eyes adjusted to the change from brightness to shade, then drew a sharp breath of satisfaction as Lefteris's voice led her across to a book-lined study. The door stood ajar, and she pushed it open.

He was leaning back in a chair with his feet on the desk while he talked on the phone, unaware of her arrival. He wore a dark blue shirt and lightweight trousers, but the casual clothes and relaxed posture did nothing to dispel the impression of sheathed power. Unlike the other rooms of the house, his office was furnished in an aggressively modern style, with all the latest technology. There was a battery of computer screens, several phones, and a fax machine on the enormous desk, all enabling him to keep in touch with his companies around the world. It was the first time Courtney had really appreciated just what a powerful man he must be, but she was in no mood to be impressed.

Stepping into the room, she shut the door with a sharp click. 'I want a word with you,' she said, too angry to care what he did to her.

He glanced over his shoulder but showed an infuriating lack of surprise at her sudden appearance. 'I'll call you back, Jeff,' he said into the phone. 'Tell Rasch that fifteen million isn't enough and let them sweat for a bit.' He put the phone down and took his feet off the desk in a leisurely way that made Courtney want to hit him.

'Is it true?' she demanded, vibrant with fury.

'Is what true?'

'That you deliberately set out to bankrupt Discovery Crete?'

He had stood up to face her but now he propped himself against his desk and folded his arms. 'Yes.'

'Yes? *Yes?*' Courtney wondered if she had heard him properly, so taken aback by his cool admission of guilt that for a long time she could only echo him incredulously. 'How dare you?' she managed at last, her eyes blue and stormy.

'I don't know why you're so surprised,' he said indifferently. 'I told you I wouldn't have you in that house.'

'I didn't think you'd go to the lengths of bankrupting the company!'

'How else was I to get you out?' he asked as if it were the most reasonable thing in the world.

Courtney felt as if she was in danger of exploding, and took several deep breaths to calm herself down. 'I can't believe you can calmly sit there and admit to it!' Unable to stand still, she paced furiously around the room. 'I can't believe you'd go to such lengths just to get even with Nikos in some stupid vendetta!'

Lefteris was watching her vivid face with narrowed eyes. 'It wasn't that difficult. All I had to do was pick up a phone,' he said, unconsciously echoing Nikos's words.

Courtney was not amused. 'How could you be so selfish, so. . .so unspeakably arrogant?' she shouted, swinging round to face him so abruptly that her plait flicked her on the cheek and she shoved it behind her shoulder again, blue eyes blazing. 'Hundreds of innocent people are going to lose their one chance of a holiday this year, thanks to you. I don't suppose you ever gave *them* a thought. Oh, no! You're rich enough to swan off whenever it suits you, so why should you care about all the people who can't? Or about everyone who works for Discovery Crete who are now out of a job—including me! And all because you can't bear to let Nikos get the better of you. I think you're despicable!'

CHAPTER FOUR

LEFTERIS lifted one eybrow, totally unimpressed by her vehemence. 'Why don't you sit down and we can discuss this rationally?'

'I don't want to sit down, and I don't feel very rational!' she snapped, glaring accusingly at him.

'Nevertheless, you can sit and listen to what I've got to say.' There was an unmistakable note of steel in his voice, and somehow Courtney found herself sitting in a chair, glowering mutely up at him. 'First,' he said, 'the chances are that your job wouldn't have lasted the summer anyway. When I made some discreet enquiries, I found out that Discovery Crete was lamentably underfunded and poorly organised. You knew that yourself. They sent you off to a dirty, dilapidated house miles from where they'd promised you'd be, in a car that should never have been allowed on the road. If you were as ignorant of Nikos's motives as you claim to be, you'd have to agree they put you in an impossible position and gave you absolutely no back-up. Hardly the actions of a professional and reputable company!'

'Nikos would have come if you hadn't been so hostile,' Courtney muttered, skulking down in her chair.

'You're very quick to defend him, aren't you?' he said coldly. 'Once you were established here, Nikos had no intention of coming near the place. Discovery Crete is just a ropey operation rigged up between him and some of his more dubious business contacts to humiliate me and make a quick killing this summer. They weren't going to care if customers complained about the conditions when they got here; they'd have their money by then and they weren't worrying about

60

a reputation for next year. All they wanted was to make a lot of money with the minimum of effort, and for Nikos it had the added bonus of rubbing my nose in the fact that he owned Villa Athina.' He stuck his hands in his pockets and looked down into Courtney's determinedly unconvinced face. 'I've got no compunction at all about pulling the rug out from beneath them. It didn't take much. If they'd been above board, they'd have been able to raise alternative finance, but nobody would touch them.'

'No, you'd made sure of that!'

'All I did was exercise a little influence in financial quarters.'

'A little influence!' Courtney echoed bitterly. 'It might be a little influence to you, but to everyone else it's utter disaster! Did you ever stop to consider what effect this vendetta of yours would have on other people? Did you ever think about the people who have paid hard-earned money for their holiday in Crete?'

Lefteris gave an exasperated sigh. 'All those who made bookings — and there weren't nearly as many as you might like to think — have been offered a full and unconditional refund, or an equivalent holiday organised by one of my own travel companies at no extra cost. Frankly,' he added, 'they'll get a much better deal that way — even if they are denied your presence as a charming hostess — and I doubt very much if I'll hear any complaints.'

'And what about those of us who've lost our jobs?' Courtney demanded, still mutinous. 'I suppose we've got no reason to complain either?'

'Any representatives here will be provided with a ticket home. That includes you, of course.'

'But I don't want to go home!' She jumped to her feet, enraged by his cool indifference. 'You know I don't! You let me work my fingers to the bone cleaning that house, and all the time you knew that you were going to bankrupt the company!'

Lefteris shrugged. 'I did warn you.'

He *had* warned her. The fact made Courtney even angrier. 'How generous of you! Do you really expect me to take your ticket and be grateful?'

'No,' he said cuttingly. 'I don't expect you to do anything that sensible, but the offer is there.'

'I'm going to stay here,' said Courtney stubbornly. 'I'm sure Nikos will let me stay in Villa Athina until I get another job.'

'You've obviously become very friendly with Nikos to be sure of that,' Lefteris said with narrowed eyes. 'Just how friendly *are* you?'

She glared at him. 'I've met him twice,' she said, tight-lipped. 'But that was enough for me to know that he was decent enough not to abandon me without a job or anywhere to stay — unlike you!'

'You should learn to be a little less hasty in your judgements, Courtney,' he said. 'I was about to offer you an alternative job.'

Courtney opened her mouth to point out that he was a fine one to talk about hasty judgements, suddenly realised what he had said, and shut it again. 'A job?' she repeated stupidly, wondering if she had heard him right. 'Why should *you* offer me a job? To ease your conscience?'

'My conscience doesn't need easing,' he said in a glacial voice. 'I have absolutely no regrets about the demise of Discovery Crete, and if you're sensible you won't either. You don't have to accept the job, but I suggest you at least listen before you throw the offer back in my face. You're unlikely to get another job here, so if you really do want to stay in Crete you'd better hear me out.'

Courtney glowered, but sank back into the chair. 'Well, what is it?' she asked ungraciously.

He sat down too, twirling his desk chair round so that he faced her. 'Katina, my housekeeper, is anxious to go back to her village to look after her mother, who isn't very well. She's going tomorrow, and although I've told her to stay as long as she wants it's very unfortunate timing, as I have a party of my European directors and their wives arriving in a few days' time. I invite members of my staff here quite regularly. It makes a break for them, and it's a useful way of getting to know them better, as well as thrashing through some common problems in a relaxed setting.'

He glanced at Courtney, who was sitting with a set face and an unusually truculent look about her mouth. She refused to look at him, but she was evidently listening. 'It occurred to me that you would be able to step into Katina's shoes and do the cooking while my guests are here,' he went on. 'I know Discovery Crete weren't the most professional company in the world, but I presume they wouldn't have given you the job unless you knew something about cooking. It doesn't have to be very grand, anyway. My directors have to sit through enough business dinners, and they like the simple meals Katina produces.'

He paused. His sharp gaze rested on Courtney's averted profile. 'Well? What do you think?'

She looked at him then, and her eyes, still bright with anger, were very direct. 'I think it's a strange offer from a man who said he didn't want anything to do with English girls,' she said frankly.

'I wouldn't offer unless it was a question of convenience. I need a cook temporarily, you need a job so that you can stay in Crete. Don't flatter yourself that it's from any secret desire for your company. You'll be in the kitchen, I'll be occupied with my guests. I don't imagine we'll need to see very much of each other.'

'And what happens if I refuse?'

He shrugged, evidently unperturbed at the prospect. 'I fly the cook over from my apartment in Athens, and you get a ticket back to London. It's more expensive and less convenient for me, but it's not an insurmountable problem. It's entirely up to you whether you stay or not.'

Her blue-grey eyes met his dark ones resentfully. 'You haven't left me much of a choice!'

'Yes, I have. You can stay here and earn enough money to spend some time by yourself afterwards, visiting the Minoan sites if that's what you really want to do. Or you can go home. You may not like the fact that I'm the one offering you the job, but don't pretend you haven't got a choice. It seems a very simple one to me.'

Courtney was silent, looking out of the window. The study faced on to a shady courtyard. Old, cracked *pithoi* cluttered one corner, their ancient elegance set off by a pot of carmine-red geraniums, and a black cat sprawled in a patch of sunlight on the hot stones. More than anything, she wanted to fling out of the room and tell Lefteris exactly what he could do with his job, but a cold voice of reason held her in her chair. He was offering her a chance to stay in Crete. Her only alternative was meekly to accept a ticket home, and if she was too hasty she might not even get that.

The cat rolled over and stretched luxuriously. 'How long would the job be for?' she asked reluctantly.

'About ten days in all. My guests arrive in four days' time, and they'll be staying a week.'

'And what happens after that?'

'You're free to go. If Katina isn't back, I'm quite capable of fending for myself, or I can move over to Athens or Paris for a while.' He hesitated. 'Feeding ten people three times a day for a week is hard work, so I'm prepared to offer you a generous salary. I imagine it would be more than enough for you to spend three or four weeks travelling by yourself.'

Courtney chewed her thumb, her eyes still on the cat, so relaxed and content in the sunshine. She didn't want to go home. She could hear what her parents would say already: 'How typical of you to get involved with a bankrupt company. We told you it wouldn't work. Ginny would never have got herself in such a mess.'

Going home would mean giving up her hope of persuading the lecturers at the interview that she really wanted to do the course. It would mean leaving Agios Giorgios behind. No more walks through the olive groves. No more Dimitra and her goat. No more poking around the cluttered shop or waving at the old men outside the *kafenion*. No more Lefteris.

She ought to be glad about *that*. If she had any principles at all, she would walk out of here and refuse to have any more to do with him, but Courtney was honest enough to admit to a shameful quiver of excitement at the prospect of being near him. He might be suspicious and arrogant and altogether hateful, but at least he wasn't boring. She might even be able to change his mind about English girls. . .

'You can have some more time to think about it, if you like,' he said, a disquieting edge of amusement in his voice as he watched the emotions warring in her expression.

'I don't need any time,' Courtney said. Her eyes met his squarely as she stood up. 'I'll take the job.'

Her bedroom faced on to the same courtyard as Lefteris's study. It was a bright and lovely room. Jasmine scrambled up the wall outside her window, and in the morning the sun slanted through the shutters and striped the cool white linen on the iron bed.

She had suggested staying in Villa Athina, but she hadn't been sorry when Lefteris had dismissed the idea and pointed out that it would be far more convenient if she slept in the house.

She woke on the first morning with a feeling of delicious lassitude, and lay for a while just blinking at the motes of dust dancing in the sunlight until she remembered exactly where she was and what she was doing there. She sat up abruptly.

Lefteris. Indignation still stirred within her whenever she thought about how ruthlessly he had disposed of Dicovery Crete. She was determined not to be grateful to him for giving her the chance to stay longer. She would do the job to the best of her ability, but she certainly wasn't going to grovel to Lefteris Markakis!

She stared at the sunlight slanting through the shutters, thinking about the strong, hawk-like face, the glossy black hair and the dark brows above that formidable nose. She thought about the unyielding strength of his body and the way his mouth curved sometimes into something that was never quite a smile. She thought about how he had kissed her, and her skin burned against the coolness of the sheet as she shifted uneasily. He was her employer now, and she was just his cook. He had made it clear that he wanted as little to do with her as possible. There was no point in remembering the dark, dangerous excitement of his touch. In another ten days or so, her job would be over. She would never have to put up with his arrogance again, and she would be free to explore Minoan ruins to her heart's content

That was what she wanted, wasn't it?

Wasn't it?

To her relief, Lefteris announced early that morning that he would be out all day, and wouldn't be returning until late. She wanted to ask whom he was having dinner with, but didn't quite dare. Was it a business contact, or one of those beautiful women who had come to the house that night? Whoever it was, she certainly wouldn't be English. She would be glamorous and sophisticated and able to spend all day getting ready for him.

Courtney suppressed a sigh, and set off to explore the house instead. It was larger even than she had imagined, stretching back and out around the courtyard. Behind the kitchen was another courtyard, which led across to the guest quarters, whitewashed like the house and decorated with the same effortlessly stylish simplicity that relied for its effect on strong colours and textures rather than gimmicks and clutter. Courtney couldn't help comparing it with her parents' immaculate, over-designed house where every last cushion had to co-ordinate.

Beyond, on the opposite side to Villa Athina, terraces stepped down to a swimming-pool which was beautifully landscaped into the hillside. Huge bushes of oleander provided privacy, but one side was left open to a spectacular view of the snow-capped mountain peaks. Courtney sat there for a while and wondered what it would be like to be a guest here. Shutting her eyes, she imagined how it would be if Lefteris didn't have that bitter prejudice against the English. How would it be if he liked her for herself and wanted to be with her? What would it be like if he had just gone inside to answer the phone and had come back, smiling, to announce that all his other guests had cancelled and they would be able to have the week together entirely alone. . .?

Her eyes snapped open. What on earth was she thinking about? The last thing she would want would be to spend a week alone with him! Getting to her feet, she headed determinedly back to the house. She was here to cook, that was all.

When Lefteris came home late that night, she was sitting at the kitchen table, reading about religion in Minoan Crete. Her cheek was propped in one hand, her hair soft and tumbled about her face and her eyes dreamy as she tried to visualise what life had been like then and she didn't at first see him watching her from the kitchen door.

'What are you doing in here at this time of night?' he demanded crossly, stalking up to stand over her as he loosened his tie.

Jerked abruptly away from Minoan Crete, Courtney ruffled up instantly, disturbed as usual by the odd mixture of nervousness and excitement he provoked. 'Where do you expect your cook to be?'

'I don't expect you to lurk in the kitchen when you're not working,' he said almost angrily.

'I thought that was precisely what I had to do!' She banged her book shut, annoyed at her own confusing reactions to him. Her heart had leapt stupidly when she had seen him striding towards her, but something about him set her on edge. 'I gathered I was to confine myself to the kitchen quarters so that you weren't contaminated by my Englishness!'

'There's no need to exaggerate,' he said irritably. To Courtney's surprise, he pulled out a chair and sat down opposite her at the table, reaching across for her book. '*Religion in Bronze Age Crete*,' he read the title, and flicked through the pages. 'So you really are interested in the Minoans!'

'It's not the kind of thing you'd make up, is it?'

'No, I suppose not.' It was the first time Courtney had ever heard him admit that he might have been wrong, and she stared across at him as he studied the book. He looked tired, she thought, and the urge to reach across and smooth the lines of strain from his face hit her so unexpectedly that she almost gasped.

He looked up suddenly from the book to find her watching him with eyes that were wide and startled and his own narrowed. 'What's the matter?'

'Nothing,' said Courtney in a husky voice, linking her hands in her lap to stop them trembling, horrified at the sudden gust of desire, the urgent need to touch him that had caught her so completely unawares. 'Nothing,' she said again sharply when his look of suspicion only deepened.

His gaze was uncomfortably penetrating, but he said only, 'Are you ready for the guests to arrive?'

She nodded, relieved at the change of subject. 'I just

need to do the shopping now, but I really need to go into Hania for that. Could I borrow your car?'

'Not after the way I've seen you driving,' he said with a sudden gleam of amusement that was nearly as unsettling as her own strange reaction to him. 'I'll take you down myself, but there's no point in going before Friday. You'll want everything fresh for their arrival on Saturday.' He shut the book and pushed it back across the table towards her, frowning down at the car keys still in his hand, as if debating something within himself, and then looked back at Courtney, sitting straight-backed and wary in her chair, her hair pushed carelessly behind her ears and her expression an odd mixture of defiance and vulnerability.

'I've got a meeting in Heraklion tomorrow,' he said gruffly. 'If you've got nothing else to do, you could come with me and I'll take you to Knossos after the meeting.'

'Knossos? Tomorrow?' Courtney looked guarded at first, taken aback by his abrupt invitation, until she realised that he really was offering her the chance to see the ruined palace she had read and dreamt about for years. What did it matter if the invitation was less than whole-hearted, or that it would mean spending a day in his uncomfortably disturbing company? Her antipathy dissolved at the prospect of seeing Knossos at long last and her blue-grey eyes lit up suddenly, transforming her face into sudden, eager beauty. 'I'd love to,' she said.

'That's arranged, then,' he said as he stood up and headed for the door. There was an odd note in his voice and Courtney wondered if he was regretting his invitation. 'We'll leave early tomorrow morning.'

After the somnolent tranquillity of Agios Giorgios, where the loudest noise was the click of the back-gammon tiles outside the *kafenion*, Heraklion battered at Courtney's ears. Traffic roared, brakes shrieked, horns blasted, pneumatic drills pummelled at concrete and assorted bangings and clatterings rose above the hubbub of chatter from the crowds jostling past on the pavement. The Greeks always seemed to talk at the tops of their voices as if they were carrying on a permanent argument, and the dawdling tourists had to shout too to make themselves heard above the racket. She heard snatches of conversation in German and French, Dutch and Italian, Swedish and English. It was all very different from Agios Giorgios, she thought wryly.

Lefteris had installed her at a table in the shade of a plane tree, and had ordered her a coffee and a *baklava*, a deliciously sticky pastry oozing honey and nuts. Courtney would have protested at the way he just ordered without even consulting her, but she was secretly glad that he hadn't left her to her own devices. The café was so busy that she was sure the waiters would have simply ignored her attempts to catch their eye; one came hurrying up as soon as Lefteris raised a finger.

Sipping her coffee now, she looked around Eleftheria Square. Heraklion might not be the loveliest of cities, but it was vibrant with life, and her spirits rose as if succumbing to the excitement in the air. Things might not have gone quite as she had expected, but she was here at last. She had wanted to see Knossos and the museum housing the fabulous collection of Minoan treasures for as long as she could remember. She still felt vaguely disloyal at having accepted a job from the man who had destroyed Discovery Crete, but if she hadn't she would be at home now, explaining to her parents what a mess she had made of things yet again. No, she had done the right thing, Courtney reassured herself. In fact, if it weren't for Lefteris, everything would be perfect.

If only he didn't make her so. . .so edgy. It wasn't anything he did, she had to admit grudgingly. It was

just something in the way he turned his head, something indefinable in the line of his mouth or the flex of
his muscles, that set the butterflies quivering deep
inside her, as if she was excited and restless and
nervous all at the same time. She didn't know what was
wrong with her. It wasn't as if she liked him. He was
an arrogant bully, a ruthless businessman who had
ruined her hard-won chance of a summer in Crete and
then condescendingly offered a couple of weeks' work
instead, expecting her to be grateful for it. No, there
was nothing to like about him.

And yet. . . Courtney licked the honey off her
fingers, her eyes resting absently on a photographer
setting up a bizarrely antiquated camera near by, still
thinking about Lefteris.

And yet he *was* taking her to Knossos. She couldn't
help feeling that he had made the invitation as if against
his better judgement, and she was sure that he was still
deeply suspicious about the fact that she was English,
but they had maintained a tacit truce as they'd driven
eastwards along the coast to Heraklion, between the
cypresses or the bright gold clumps of broom that lined
the road.

He had made no disparaging comments and she had
been careful to say nothing that he might misinterpret.
He had even opened up enough to tell her something
about himself. He tried to spend the summer living
simply in Crete, he told her, but for the rest of the year
he travelled between Athens and New York, London
and Paris, Rome and the Far East. . . Courtney could
imagine him running a world-wide operation, dealing
in millions as casually as pennies, brushing aside rivals
or squashing upstart companies that dared to challenge
him the way Discovery Crete had done. The only
puzzle was why a man like that would bother to take a
girl he despised to Knossos.

In the end, Courtney had decided to stop worrying
and just make the most of her opportunity, but she had

been very conscious of him sitting beside her, and her eyes had kept sliding over to his hands on the steering-wheel, or his profile as he watched the road ahead. She had tried to concentrate on the sun glinting on the deep blue sea instead, but the next moment her gaze would drift over towards him again and she would wonder, as she had once before, what it would be like if he smiled at her and assured her that he was taking her simply because he wanted to be with her.

'Courtney?'

Wrapped up in her thoughts, she started violently when Lefteris materialised in front of her a few minutes later. The sudden sight of him drove the breath from her lungs as effectively as a punch in the stomach, and she put her glass down on the table so jerkily that water slopped everywhere. 'Oh, it's you,' she said weakly.

'You were miles away,' he said, an undercurrent of amusement, and something else she couldn't identify, in his voice. 'What were you thinking about?'

Not daring to look at him in case he read the truth in her eyes, she stared desperately at the passing crowd for inspiration. 'I — er — I was just trying to guess people's nationalities,' she improvised. 'That family over there *must* be French, don't you think? No one else wears clothes with quite that style. I wonder if I'm as easy to identify?'

Lefteris studied her. She was wearing another of her old dresses that was soft and comfortable and not at all smart. It had been a deep blue once, but the colour had faded until it was almost exactly that of her eyes. Walking up and down the road to Agios Giorgios had given her skin a glow of gold, and the brown hair fell softly to her shoulders, thick and streaky with sunshine.

'You look very English to me,' he said slowly.

Courtney unslung her bag from the back of the chair and stood up. 'Coming from you, that's not exactly a compliment, is it? In your eyes, all English girls are cold, manipulative and immoral.'

'I wouldn't call you cold,' he said, deliberately not acquitting her of the other two accusations. He dropped some money on to the table, and glanced at her with that odd expression in his eyes again. 'Not knowing the way you kiss.'

The colour surged into Courtney's face and she turned quickly away so that he wouldn't guess how her heart was lurching and jolting against her ribs. Why did he have to remind her about that wretched kiss? It wasn't as if she needed any reminding. Her mind could still replay it in perfect, humiliating detail, and the last thing she wanted was to know that Lefteris remembered it too. The least he could have done to atone was to pretend that it had never happened, but no! Just when she was wondering if she might not quite like him after all, he had to go and remind her of just how arrogant and despicable he really was!

She kept her face averted as they walked across the square to the famous Archaeological Museum. Lefteris had promised her a visit if there was time before they went on to Knossos, and it seemed as if he had not forgotten. Courtney had spent years longing to see its famous treasures, but now that she was actually there all she could think about was Lefteris and how he had kissed her. Her resentment grew as she moved from case to case, staring unseeingly down at the exhibits.

Why, why, why had he mentioned that kiss? Here she was at last, standing in front of the famous bull's head with its gilded horns and grave, powerful gaze; here was the snake goddess, and the ivory acrobat, caught in mid-leap over the bull's back, muscles taut and veins standing out with tension; here was the unique clay disc from Phaestos with its mysterious inscriptions, its indecipherable message from the past. . .She ought to be drinking it all in, not wasting this precious opportunity remembering how warm his hands had been, how exciting his mouth.

It wasn't fair.

It was cool and quiet inside the museum. Clusters of visitors moved around them, speaking in the hushed tone common to churches and museums, whatever the language, only the hectoring, lecturing voices of the guides rising above the murmur. Courtney barely noticed them as she bent over the cases with feverish concentration, while Lefteris's presence simmered distractingly at the edge of her mind. She found herself riveted by his finger, pointing out the detail on a vase, or his body, leaning next to hers as they peered into a case of sealstones.

She stared resentfully at a group of figurines with remarkably carved faces, some serene, some grotesque, others simply exuding an individual character that shone across four thousand years. She was angry with herself, furious with Lefteris for being able to distract her so easily.

'This one always reminds me of Dimitra,' he said, appearing so suddenly at her shoulder that she had to supress a gasp at his nearness. He gave one of his rare smiles as he pointed at a carving of an old woman whose mouth was open as if she had been caught in mid-sentence, and Courtney wondered if it was really possible that he didn't realise how he was affecting her.

With an effort, she brought her attention away from his smile to the carving. It was, indeed, so like Dimitra that she giggled, forgetting her tension for a moment. 'She's very voluble, isn't she?'

'You seem to have made a big hit with her,' he commented as they moved on to the next case. 'I stopped to talk to her on my way down to Hania yesterday, and she seemed to know more about you than I did!'

'I used to meet her whenever I went down to Agios

Giorgios,' Courtney explained. 'She's teaching me Greek.'

'Oh? And how are you progressing?'

'Quite well,' she said proudly. 'I can talk about the weather a bit, and ask after her arthritis and her goat.'

'That should come in handy next time you stop to chat to goats,' he said with another glinting, sidelong smile. 'Perhaps you'll get more response next time!'

She opened her mouth to protest at the way he kept reminding her of how ridiculous she had been, but when she looked into his eyes she realised how absurd she must have looked, and inexplicably she found herself smiling back at him, sharing the humour of the memory without the hostility or the tension.

The wooden display cases and the murmuring tourists faded unnoticed into the background as their smiles caught and held and deepened until, as if simultaneously remembering how much they disliked and distrusted each other, they both turned abruptly away.

Courtney's pulse was thumping as he led the way up the stairs to the upper gallery. He had smiled at her, really smiled, as if he liked her! She glanced at him out of the corner of her eye as they walked slowly along the gallery, pretending to admire the exuberant frescoes. His smile had vanished. Instead, he was frowning at the celebrated fresco of the Minoan priestess nicknamed 'La Parisienne'. The smile hadn't meant anything to him. If anything, he had probably just been remembering how utterly ridiculous she had looked, standing half naked on an empty hillside excusing herself to a goat.

She *had* been ridiculous, Courtney realised dolefully. She still was. What could be more ridiculous than getting herself into a state just because he had smiled at her? Nothing had changed.

Still, she felt stupidly shy and awkward as they made their way out of the museum into the glare and bustle of Eleftheria Square once more, and could only nod

dumbly when Lefteris suggested lunch before they went
to Knossos.

He took her to a small taverna outside the city. They
sat outside on the terrace, and the sun filtered through
the vines, throwing elegant shadows on the white
tablecloth. Courtney watched the clashing pink and red
geraniums stacked along the wall and wondered how it
was possible to be so aware of Lefteris's every movement when she wasn't even looking at him.

She never forgot the simple, delicious meal they
shared at that quiet taverna. The bustling city and the
tourists teeming over Knossos might have been a
million miles away. They ate slices of *mizithra*, a soft
curd cheese made from goat's milk, with thick pieces
of bread and fat, wrinkled olives. After that came
plates of roast lamb, hauntingly flavoured with thyme
and oregano, and a cool, crisp salad made with cucumbers, onions and sweet red tomatoes, all glistening
with olive oil.

She was agonisingly conscious of Lefteris, and
wished desperately that she could regain the antagonism that had slipped away so unaccountably when she
had been unable to resist the smile in his eyes. It was
easier to talk to him when she was hating him. He, too,
seemed aware of a new awkwardness between them, a
constraint that had never existed before, and they were
both very careful not to touch as they wandered around
Knossos that afternoon.

In silence, they walked through the ruins of the once
mighty palace, gazing up at the reconstructed frescos
and climbing great sweeps of steps. Courtney was
disappointed at first. She had pictured a vast complex,
peopled with the glamorous Minoans, whose gaiety
and sophistication were so obvious from the treasures
in the museum. She had thought there would be a real
sense of a palace that had been made for a pleasure-
loving lifestyle and the more violent, sinister rituals
that were its darker side, but the brightly dressed

crowds criss-crossing the central court seemed to have
destroyed the magic, the ghosts of the spectacular bull-
leaping rituals banished in a babel of languages and the
ubiquitous whirr of the video camera.

CHAPTER FIVE

LEFTERIS read the disappointment in her face and led her away from the central area to a quiet corner in the shade of the pine trees that surrounded the site. Here there were narrow corridors turning abruptly into dark, windowless rooms, sudden steps and confusing dead ends. Courtney ran her fingers along the ancient stones. The light was blocked into brilliance and deep shade, and whenever she risked a glance at Lefteris he seemed outlined in extraordinary clarity. It was quiet away from the crowds and the sense of the past was much stronger. Wandering from room to room, she found herself hesitating in doorways, her feet crunching on the pine needles that lay thickly on the stones, and glancing over her shoulder as if she might catch a glimpse of one of the figures she had seen at the museum, slipping silently between sunlight and shadow.

'It's almost spooky, isn't it?' she confessed to him as they sat on the edge of the roof that had been built to cover the Hall of Double Axes, looking down on stone walls which were all that was left of the maze of little rooms and corridors. Far in the distance, at the end of the valley, they could just see the sea between the hills, a deep, glinting blue below the horizon. A Minoan might have looked at exactly the same view, Courtney thought with a shiver that was part pleasure, part awe. Her gaze came back to the crumbled walls beneath them. 'Why do you think they made it so confusing?' she asked. 'Why go to all the trouble of making all those different levels, and those corridors that don't seem to lead anywhere?'

'Who knows?' said Lefteris. 'When it was all roofed,

it must have been even more difficult to find your way around. You can see how easily the myth of the labyrinth would have grown up around a place like this.'

As if to prove his point, a puzzled tourist stopped almost immediately beneath them. Unaware of his audience, he stood turning his guidebook round and round as he tried to work out what he was supposed to be looking at. Scratching his head, he gave up and walked off, still holding his book upside-down.

Courtney and Lefteris watched him go, and then glanced at each other. Involuntarily, they both smiled, and the brittle tension dissolved into a new and much more disturbing awareness. She had the strangest feeling, as if everything had suddenly deepened in intensity. The sky seemed somehow bluer, the light more luminous. She spread her hands on the warm stone and felt his smile seeping through her, a deep, tingling warmth. The air smelt of pines and little sparrows chittered around them on the old stones, oblivious to the past.

'Tell me the story of the labyrinth,' she said suddenly.

'Surely you know that story?' he said in surprise.

'I do, but I'd like to hear it, here in Knossos.' She glanced at him. The light bouncing off the stones threw the fine bones of her face into sharp relief, and her eyes reflected the deep cobalt-blue of the sky. 'Do you mind?'

He looked away, as if with an effort. 'No, I don't mind,' he said, a curious undercurrent in his voice. He was silent for a while, his gaze fixed on the sea in the distance, and then he began. 'Once there was a mighty king called Minos who commanded all the seas around Crete, and lived in a great palace that was the wonder of all who saw it. The splendour of the court at Knossos was legendary, but there was a darker side to it, too. Minos's wife, Pasiphae, had given birth to a monster, half-bull, half-man, called the Minotaur. This was such a terrifying beast that it had to be confined in an endless labyrinth below the palace, and placated by a dreadful tribute. Every nine years, the Athenians had to choose seven youths and seven maidens who were delivered into the heart of the labyrinth. It was so confusing that, once inside, they couldn't possibly find their way out, and they roamed helplessly through the dark corridors where the Minotaur waited to devour them one by one.'

Courtney shivered. 'It must have been terrifying. You can just imagine them, can't you? Lost in the darkness, coming up against blank walls, never knowing if the monster was going to be waiting around the next corner. . .it's a disturbing story, isn't it?'

'Yes, but it *is* just a story,' he said, amused by her grimace. 'It probably grew up from nothing more than the fact that visitors here were overwhelmed by the complexity of the palace.'

Courtney decided she preferred the horror to his prosaic explanation. 'Go on with the story,' he said.

'Well, there was terrible grief in Athens every time the tribute was due, and every family feared that their own child might be taken, until the king's son, Theseus, swore that he would put an end to their fear. He announced that he would take his place among those sent to the labyrinth, and that he would kill the Minotaur. Naturally, his father, King Aegeus, didn't want him to go, but Theseus was insistent, and they set off in a ship with black sails of mourning. He was fortunate, too, that King Minos's daughter, Ariadne, fell in love with him when she saw him arriving at Knossos. She said she would help him, if he would promise to marry her and take her to Athens. Theseus promised, of course, and she gave him a ball of thread so that he could unwind it as he went into the labyrinth, and follow it back to the entrance when he had killed the Minotaur. And that is what happened. Theseus, in the way of heroes, slew the monster, and escaped with all the Athenians, and Ariadne.

'Unfortunately,' Lefteris went on, 'the story didn't have the happy ending stories like that are supposed to have. Theseus abandoned Ariadne while she lay sleeping on a beach on the island of Naxos, and sailed back to Athens without her. He had arranged with his father that if he was returning alive he would signal the good news in advance by changing the black sails to white, but in all the excitement he forgot. King Aegeus, watching anxiously for his return from a cliff-top at Cape Sounion, saw the black sails and knew that it meant his son was dead. In his grief, he threw himself into the sea, which has been known as the Aegean ever since, so instead of returning to great rejoicing Theseus was met by the news that his father had died because of his own forgetfulness.'

'It served him right for the way he treated poor Ariadne,' said Courtney. 'He used her, and when he didn't need her any more he just left her on her own.'

'That kind of behaviour isn't limited to ancient myths,' Lefteris said, his expression bitter. 'Or, indeed, to men.'

The thought seemed to make him withdraw and they were silent as they drove home, with the sea still and silver on their right, and the hills an ethereal blue-grey in the evening light. Courtney wondered whom he had been thinking of when he had looked so bitter. Was it Linda, his brother's wife, who had somehow contributed to the enmity between him and Nikos, or was it someone else? She tried to imagine a girl who would leave Lefteris, a girl he must have loved for him still to feel her betrayal. How could she have done it?

She glanced across at him, remembering how deep and warm his voice had been as he'd told her that old, old story, remembering how the shadows had fallen across his face, and she felt suddenly hollow inside, as if her stomach had simply disappeared.

The confusing turns and unexpected dead ends of
the labyrinthine walls at Knossos were an apt symbol
of her feelings for him, she thought wryly. Just when
she thought she disliked him intensely, he would do
something unfair, like smile, and she would be stopped
in her tracks and have to change her mind. Resentment
would suddenly turn into gratitude, awkwardness into
desire, indignation into liking. . .now she didn't know
how she felt about him. She was lost in the labyrinth
and didn't know what she would find at its centre.

Or did she?

Courtney's mind shied nervously away from the
thought that her feelings for Lefteris might be leading
her into something far more dangerous than mere
liking. His guests were arriving the day after tomorrow,
and he would have no time for her then. She would be
taken up with cooking, and in just over a week's time
she would say goodbye to him. He hadn't said anything
about her staying on after his guests had left. Why
should he? He had never pretended to feel anything
but contempt for her, and she was the one who had
said she wanted to leave Agios Giorgios and spend her
time poking around Minoan ruins.

That *was* what she wanted. Of course it was.

The next morning, Lefteris announced that he would
drive her down to the market in Hania that evening,
when everything opened after the afternoon siesta, and
promptly disappeared into his office where Courtney
could hear him making long phone calls in a sharp,
decisive voice.

Left with nothing to do but make lunch, she walked
down into Agios Giorgios to get some fresh bread. She
was glad of the excuse to get out of the house. The
atmosphere between them was subtly different, less
hostile but somehow more disturbing. One more week,
Courtney reminded herself for the umpteenth time.
Don't do anything stupid.

Dimitra was sitting by the roadside, holding her goat by its long tether while it browsed contentedly behind her. She greeted Courtney warmly as she came down the road, and they ran through her repertoire of Greek phrases, before Dimitra launched into a voluble speech, in which a bewildered Courtney could recognise only Lefteris's name repeated several times. Seeing that she had lost her, Dimitra began again, this time with an elaborate pantomime.

'Ah!' said Courtney as it finally clicked. 'Yes, I've moved into Lefteris's house while Katina is away. I'm his cook.'

Not surprisingly, this was lost in Dimitra, so she launched into her own pantomime, which got a little involved as she tried to explain about Katina's mother being ill. Dimitra watched her with interest, but to Courtney's surprise she beamed and began patting her heart. At first, Courtney wondered if she thought Katina's mother had had a heart attack, but when Dimitra kept repeating Lefteris's name and pointing at Courtney it dawned on her at last that Dimitra thought they were lovers.

'No!' she said with burning cheeks. 'Lefteris and I . . .no,' she tried urgently, and when this seemed to have no effect on Dimitra's grin she summoned up her Greek. 'No, no,' she said again. '*Ne, ne, ne!*'

'*Ne,*' Dimitra confirmed with a kindly smile that said she understood.

Relieved, Courtney waved goodbye and walked on into the village. Thank heavens she had been able to put a stop to *that* idea! The bakery was crowded, and she listened idly to the machine-gun chatter of conversation, trying to pick out words she recognised, like *ne* and——

Courtney's thoughts broke off as appalled realisation struck. In her determination to correct Dimitra of her misapprehension, she had made the most elementary mistake of all. *Ne* didn't mean no, as it surely ought to. It meant yes.

Squirming, Courtney remembered Dimitra's knowing smile. She must have thought she was only too eager to admit to being involved with Lefteris! As if in a dream, she bought two loaves and stepped outside into the bright street, clutching the bread to her in horror. What had she done?

Unsure of why it was so important to let Dimitra understand how wrong she had been, Courtney walked anxiously along the road, peering through the olives and up the hillsides, but there was no sign of the old woman. She even retraced her steps to Dimitra's house, but there was no one there except the fat hens. In the end, she gave up and went slowly back to the villa, stupidly reluctant to face Lefteris.

Fortunately, he was still shut in his study, which gave her time to compose herself while she made the lunch. Really, it was nothing to get worked up about, she reasoned as she stuffed huge, sweet tomatoes with rice and onions and some of the dried herbs Katina kept hanging from a beam in the kitchen. It was a perfectly ordinary mistake that anyone could have made. There was absolutely nothing to feel embarrassed about.

When the tomatoes were cooked she took them out of the oven and set them on the table with the bread she had bought and a hunk of *psilotiri*, a strong, hard cheese made only from the milk of goats grazed on the highest Cretan mountains. She had bought some of the wild greens that most people gathered for themselves from the hillsides. Courtney often saw them carrying huge bundles of leaves down the road, but hadn't dared try foraging for herself. Safer by far, she thought, to buy them from the shop, even if it was less authentic. They still made a lovely side-dish, just boiled and tossed in olive oil and lemon juice.

Lefteris looked preoccupied when he emerged from his office, but he cast a glance of surprised approval at the table as he sat down. 'Have you been cooking all morning?'

'I went down to the village as well.' Courtney looked down at her plate and drew a breath. It was now or never! 'Actually, I did something rather stupid while I was down there.'

'Oh?' He sounded resigned rather than surprised as he cut himself a piece of cheese.

She cleared her throat. 'You remember I was telling you how well I was getting on with my Greek?'

He looked up at that. 'Yes?'

'Well, I met Dimitra this morning.' Having begun easily enough, Courtney suddenly found it more and more difficult to continue. 'She seemed to know all about my moving in here, but for some reason she thinks that you and I. . .that we. . .'

'That we what?'

'You know. . .' Courtney's cheeks were scarlet, and Lefteris's eyes sharpened, though whether with annoyance or amusement or something quite different it was impossible to tell.

'She thinks we're lovers?'

'Yes.' She exhaled a sharp breath, glad that she hadn't had to say the word herself. 'It's a ridiculous idea, of course,' she said, trying to laugh off her embarrassment.

'Ridiculous,' he agreed, but there was an odd note in his voice. 'What did you do to give Dimitra the idea in the first place?'

'I didn't do anything! She just seemed to have it in her head. I tried to tell her how wrong she was, but I got a bit muddled up, and kept saying *ne*, meaning no, so now she must think it's true.'

Courtney hung her head guiltily, expecting him to be furious, but when she risked a glance at him she saw an unexpected grin tugging at the corner of his mouth. It made him look much younger, much less fierce and disquietingly attractive.

'I suppose it's an easy mistake to make,' was all he said.

She stared at him in amazement, baffled by his reaction. 'I thought I'd better tell you,' she said at last. 'I didn't think you'd want everyone in the village thinking that I was your girlfriend. You're the one who keeps banging on about how ghastly English girls are, and I'd hate your reputation to suffer!'

'It sounds as if the damage has already been done,' he said, ignoring her sarcasm. 'I don't quite see what you expect me to do about it.'

'I thought you could make it clear to Dimitra exactly what our relationship is,' she said, conscious that she sounded sullen.

He leant back in his chair and regarded Courtney thoughtfully. 'And what *is* our relationship?'

'I'm your cook.' She steeled herself to meet his dark eyes squarely. 'Your temporary cook,' she stressed. 'And you're my employer.'

'Your temporary employer,' he corrected her. 'So you want me to tell Dimitra that we haven't got a relationship, and if we did it would only be a temporary one?' There was no mistaking the mockery in his voice and Courtney felt her hackles rise.

'Yes, that's what I want,' she said firmly.

Even so, she spent a ridiculous amount of time getting ready to go to Hania. She kept fiddling with her hair, plaiting it, deciding it didn't suit her, letting it down and deciding *that* looked too much as if she was making an effort to look nice. Her hair had always been too mousy for it to matter much how she wore it before, but now that it was bleached with golden streaks of sunshine it really *did* look much better tumbling soft and thick to her shoulders. Did Lefteris think so?

Courtney leant forward and stared at herself in the mirror, wondering how he saw her. Blue-grey eyes stared back at her through their fringe of dark lashes.

They had always been her best feature, even if they did look hopelessly dreamy next to Ginny's sparkling green ones. Otherwise, there was really nothing special about her: a straight little nose, a soft mouth, fine skin. . .no, there was nothing wrong with her exactly. There was just nothing particularly striking either. There was certainly nothing to attract a man like Lefteris Markakis.

Suppressing a sigh, Courtney turned away from the mirror. What did it matter, anyway? She pulled on a dress patterned with muted blues and greys and fastened a blue suede belt around her waist. The dress was made of a soft, silky sort of cotton, and it whispered against her bare legs as she walked to the car with Lefteris.

She had found him in the hall, checking his trouser pockets for the car keys. He wore dark trousers and a plain white shirt with a tie, and his jacket was slung over one shoulder. He'd glanced up at the sound of her footsteps and Courtney had wished suddenly that she had put on her old jeans and kept her hair firmly plaited. In spite of sleeves rolled up to the elbow, the white shirt and tie had a formality that suited his strong features. In a peculiar way it emphasised the latent power of his body far more than the dark, traditional outfit he had worn while hunting.

He looked unnervingly attractive as he held open the door of the car for her. Courtney got in, her senses quivering with a new and unsettling awareness. Everything seemed unnaturally vivid: the feel of the soft material of her dress curving over her breasts and the hard plastic of the door-handle beneath her fingers; the smell of the upholstery mingling with the lingering scent of orange blossom from the garden; the solid strength of Lefteris beside her and his long fingers on the car key as he started the engine. Even that seemed louder than usual.

Courtney cleared her throat. She really must pull herself together.

As they turned off the track on to the road, they met Dimitra, looking rather lop-sided without her goat, evidently on her way to move her little flock of sheep instead. 'I suppose I'd better have a word with her,' Lefteris said with a sardonic look. 'Since you're so anxious to convince her that you're not madly in love with me!'

Crimson with mortification, Courtney sat chewing her lip while he and Dimitra embarked on one of those intense, argumentative-sounding conversations the Cretans seemed to specialise in. At length, Dimitra patted him on the arm, peered round him to give Courtney a broad, gap-toothed smile, and stepped back with a parting comment that left him with a peculiar expression on his face.

'What did she say?' Courtney asked suspiciously as he put the car into gear and drove on.

'I suspect you'd rather not know,' he said in a dry voice.

'I'd rather not *not* know!'

He hesitated, then shrugged. 'If you must know, she said that we can deny it all we want, but she still thinks your first answer was the right one.'

Feeling the vivid colour stain her cheeks, she turned her face away. 'How. . .how ridiculous,' she said weakly.

The covered market in Hania was built in the shape of a cross, and bustled and jostled with enough life and colour to divert her for a while from the business of untangling exactly how she felt about Lefteris. Fish were laid out on slabs, wet and glistening, while their heads lay casually discarded on the floor below. Courtney recognised the distinctive spikes of swordfish, and a stallholder, noticing her interest, gestured proudly to his display of bream and mullet, squid and cuttlefish, and the octopus strung above them.

Further on, they found boxes of fruit and vegetables, a riot of colour and freshness. There were great piles of oranges, ripe tomatoes, cucumbers and courgettes so fresh that they still had flowers. There were glossy purple aubergines and the bright red and green of fresh peppers. There were crisp lettuces and vine leaves and boxes of different kinds of *horta*, the wild greens gathered on the hillsides outside Hania. Courtney wandered up and down the aisle, inspecting piles of artichokes and melons, boxes of kumquats, strings of garlic and sacks of the more humble onions and potatoes. Averting her eyes from the baskets seething with live snails, she pulled out her list and wondered where to begin.

Lefteris was a surprisingly patient interpreter and the familiar tension between them evaporated as she nosed melons and turned over tomatoes with a professional hand, and he accepted the stallholders' obvious joshing at his unaccustomedly lowly role as bag carrier with good humour. Laden down with fruit and vegetables, they moved on to buy cheese in a narrow shop where they had to squeeze between enormous cheeses stacked one on top of the other. The smiling woman gave Courtney little pieces of Cretan specialities to try while Lefteris watched, amused at her intent expression. *Graviera*, *mizithra*, *staka*, *malaka*. . .Courtney found herself smiling back as she repeated the names after him like an incantation.

There were bread shops and butchers and delicatessens and a kiosk in the middle where Courtney, guiltily aware of how belated it would be, bought a postcard to send to her parents. Best of all, though, were the stalls that sold herbs and spices. Great bunches of dried herbs hung from the ceiling and were stacked in plastic bags at the front where she could read their names and how they were used. Many seemed to have as much a medicinal use as a culinary one. Dittany tea was good for the stomach and headaches, *kiparisaki* — whatever that was — for the kidneys. Courtney's face was bright with delight as she picked up bags of cinnamon and cumin and coriander, camomile and oregano, marjoram and the twiggy branches of *malotira*, and sniffed at them, enjoying their pungent aromas. She couldn't resist the jars of Cretan honey, made by bees fed on thyme and wild flowers, or the sacks of nuts and huge bowls of olives. Baskets were strung up above spectacular displays of wreaths carved with elaborate motifs of fruit and flowers and leaves. Courtney assumed that they were wooden until Lefteris told her they were made of bread, baked hard.

'Traditonally, they're given to guests at a wedding,' he said. 'I suspect these ones are bought mainly by tourists. Many of the old traditions are dying out, some of them for the better. Cretan weddings used to be a lot more dramatic than they are today. It used to be quite common for brides to be abducted from rival villages and married out of hand.' He glanced down at Courtney's vivid face. 'You'll be glad to know that stealing brides is definitely a habit that has died out!'

For a dangerous moment, she allowed herself to wonder what it would be like if Lefteris snatched her up and refused to allow her to leave Agios Giorgios. She stared at a heart-shaped carving. 'That's one thing I don't have to worry about, then,' she said, and was horrified at how wistful her voice sounded. 'Fortunately!' she added hastily.

She had expected that once the shopping was done they would go straight home, but when they had stacked the bags in the back of the car Lefteris glanced at his watch. 'It's a little early to eat,' he said. 'I may as well show you something of Hania.'

Courtney wasn't sorry for the opportunity to explore. He led her past smart shops that wouldn't have been out of place in Paris or Milan, and down narrow, tortuous back streets that were full of derelict charm. The Venetian houses must have been grand once, but

now their plaster had faded and flaked, and there were
television aerials and drooping wires everywhere. They
were still stylish, though, Courtney decided, with their
dark, secretive doorways and the elegant wrought-iron
balconies.

Walking beside Lefteris down the confusion of alley-
ways, she told herself that her light heart had nothing
to do with his company. It was just that she liked
dilapidated places like this, which had none of the
aggressive design her parents so favoured. She liked
the cats weaving between the balcony railings, and the
weeds and wild flowers growing out of a tumbledown
wall. It was a surprisingly private place. Every now and
then, they would get a glimpse of a dim interior with a
flickering television, or the suggestion of a tangled
garden hidden behind a high wall. Bicycles were
propped against doorways, and someone's washing-up
dried in a small window. She liked the pots of geraniums marching up crumbling steps, and the smiling
boys weaving past on their scooters.

Most of all, she liked the brush of Lefteris's body as
they stepped to one side to let someone past, and the
touch of his fingers on her arm as he pointed out an
ornate doorknocker or a man casually carrying a huge
terracotta pot that might have come from Knossos.

Think about leaving, Courtney reminded herself
desperately, but it was as if the gathering darkness held
her in thrall and all she could think about was the curve
of his mouth and the line of his cheek and the way her
senses thrilled whenever he touched her.

They emerged on to the harbour front as if into
another world. After the quiet back streets, it seemed
as if half of Europe was there, strolling up and down
the quayside past the restaurants with their striped
awnings and beckoning waiters. Even in such a crowd,
Lefteris stood out, Courtney thought, sliding a sidelong
glance at him. He had loosened his tie, and his jacket
was slung casually over his shoulder. She wondered if

he noticed how many women turned their heads surreptitiously to eye his powerful frame and distinctive
features. Among the uncomfortably dressed tourists in
their shorts and sandals, he moved with a balanced
ease, a fighter's controlled tread.

He took her to a shabby taverna at the far end of the
harbour, where it was quiet and dark and few tourists
bothered to explore. He was greeted like a long-lost
son, and Courtney found herself ushered ceremoni-
ously to a table in the corner. She watched Lefteris
joking with the proprietor, startled as always by how
much younger he looked when he laughed. He was
utterly at home in this tiny taverna with its hot,
clattering kitchen and plastic tablecloths, but she could
imagine him just as easily in some exclusive French
restaurant. He was a man at home in any situation, she
decided. His assurance and authority were simply part
of him, and he carried them wherever he went.

After an animated discussion, the proprietor brought
them a bottle of wine from a Hania vineyard, and
Lefteris poured it into the glasses, his face intent as he
watched the wine. It was easier to look at him when
his eyes were lowered, and Courtney's eyes drifted
from the thick, dark lashes, down the straight nose to
his mouth. Something insistent began to beat deep
inside her. Terrified that her hands might reach across
the table to touch him of their own accord, she seized
her glass.

'Cheers!' she croaked.

'*Yiammas*!' He was smiling. Didn't he know what his
smile did to her? He touched his glass to hers. 'You
must always chink glasses before you drink,' he said.

'Why's that?'

'We've been making wine in Crete for over six
thousand years,' he said, 'so some of our superstitions
are very old. The ancient Greeks worshipped the vine,
and they believed that to be truly appreciated wine
should be savoured with all five senses. Taste is

obvious, and of course you feel the touch of the wine on your tongue.' Holding up his glass to the light, he swirled the wine round and then bent his head to sniff it. 'You can admire the colour with your eyes and smell the bouquet. We chink our glasses so that we can appreciate with our ears, and ensure that all our senses are satisfied.

It didn't take a glass of wine to make her senses work overtime when he was around, Courtney thought ruefully, but she laughed and clinked her glass against his obediently. '*Yiammas!*' she repeated.

Over the glasses their eyes met for a jarring moment, and their smiles faded at the same time. 'Er—what's on the menu?' she asked quickly, dropping her gaze.

'We'd better go and see.' To her surprise, he led her out to the kitchen. She had expected the staff to resent this sudden invasion, but they all seemed to think it was perfectly normal, and the proprietor beamed as he pulled big aluminium dishes out of the warming oven for her to inspect. There was a tray of appetising stuffed vegetables—aubergines, courgettes, artichokes and tomatoes—all lined up neatly, a casserole of squid, lamb cutlets cooked with herbs and wrapped in paper packets, okra in a thick tomato sauce and a deliciously oily stew made with potatoes, onions and tomatoes. Courtney sniffed at it appreciatively but changed her mind when she discovered that it was cooked with snails, and opted for a stuffed aubergine instead.

'You're very quiet,' Lefteris said when they were back at the table. 'Are you all right?'

No, she wasn't. She felt jittery, on edge, and the insistent pounding along her veins was making it impossible to concentrate. She fiddled with her fork. 'I was just thinking that I don't really know anything about you,' she said. It was true, even if it wasn't a strictly accurate answer.

'You know I'm a businessman.'

'I don't mean how you make your money. I mean the important things about you.'

His eyes flickered. 'Like what?'

'Well, your family, for instance.'

He swirled the wine around in his glass and shrugged. 'We're a Cretan family,' he said as if that explained everything. 'My grandfather was born in Villa Athina, and his grandfather before him. My roots are deep in the Cretan mountains, but my father was ambitious. He went to America and built up the company from nothing, but as children we always knew that Crete was our home. It was my father who built the house I live in now, and he made sure we spent at least every summer there so that we would never forget who we were and where we belonged.

'After my father died, I took over the company. It's expanded out of all recognition since then, but I have tried to keep to the principles he established, and Agios Giorgios is still the centre of the family. My sisters come every summer and let their families run riot.'

'What about your brother? You said he married an English girl?'

'Linda.' The name seemed to stick in his throat. 'Yes, Christos married Linda, and lived to regret it. She was a beautiful girl, but rotten to the core. All she cared about was money. You might not have heard of the Markakis name, but she certainly had. Christos met her in London, and she played it very carefully, making sure they were safely married before he brought her home to meet his family. I'm not quite sure what she was expecting, but it certainly wasn't Agios Giorgios. She wanted to be part of the jet-set and lie around in luxury all day; instead she got the mountains, a quiet village and a lot of olive trees. She'd only been there a day before she started nagging Christos to take her away to the bright lights.'

'Is that why she went back to England?' Courtney

found it hard to imagine wanting to leave Agios Giorgios now.

'One of the reasons.' Lefteris's face closed. 'Christos was killed in a car crash a few months later. She couldn't wait to take her money and run.'

'I'm sorry,' said Courtney awkwardly. 'I can see now why you don't like English girls.'

'I blame myself,' he said abruptly. 'I should have done more to prevent the marriage. I knew exactly what English girls were like. I considered marrying one once myself, until I found out that her love depended entirely on how many millions you could offer her. I was very young at that time, and the company wasn't nearly as large as it is now. Sabrina kept me hanging on a string for a time, but when it came down to it she opted for someone much older and much richer than I was then. Never mind that it meant breaking up his marriage and making his life a misery until he divorced her with several million as a settlement. All that mattered to Sabrina—like Linda—was what she got out of it. Unlike you, they thought that money was the only thing that had any importance at all. I had a lucky escape.'

If he had been as young as he said, he would also have been desperately hurt. Courtney stared down into her wine. 'Is she the reason you've never married? Don't you want a family of your own?'

'Some day, yes, but Christos's experience taught me that marriage isn't worth the price unless you're absolutely sure you've found the right woman.'

'And you haven't found her?' Courtney was still studying her wine.

'No.' He broke off some bread and looked across at her. Her lowered lashes cast shadows on her cheeks. 'Not yet.'

CHAPTER SIX

THERE was a long, intense silence. Courtney could feel his eyes on her face as she twisted the glass between her fingers. She looked at her plate, at the battered cruet set, at the poster of Switzerland which someone had stuck on the wall for some reason, at anything except Lefteris.

'You know about me now,' he said at last. 'What about you? You haven't told me about your family.'

'I'm a bit of a misfit.' Courtney picked at her aubergine, wondering if he could ever understand what it was like to be surrounded by confident, capable people when you were neither. 'My parents are both very clever, both successful in their own fields. They're never muddled, like me. Things seem obvious to them. They're always confident they know best, and they always do. It's very hard to argue with people who are always right. They just. . .*overwhelm* you. I wanted to please them, but I always seemed to end up disappointing them instead. Sometimes I think they wonder where on earth I came from. My sister has always been a credit to them, but I'm like a cuckoo in the nest.'

'Are you like your sister?'

'Like Ginny?' The idea was so absurd that Courtney almost laughed. She laid down her fork, remembering years of being urged to be more like her sister. 'No, I'm not like her. She's everything I'm not. Ginny's beautiful and I'm ordinary. She's clever and witty, and I'm quiet and shy. She's sensible, I'm a dreamer. Everything she does, she does perfectly, whereas I just seem to make a mess of things. I grew up feeling hopelessly inadquate because I could never be like her. while Ginny was out winning scholarships and tennis championships, I was reading in my room. That's where I learnt to love history so much. It always seemed so much easier than coping with my parents' ambitions.'

'Why didn't you go on to study history, if that's what you were so interested in?' he asked.

'I'd got so used to feeling hopeless that I just seized up as soon as the word exam was mentioned, and in the end my teachers despaired of me. After I left school, my parents decided that I might as well do a cookery course, as it was the only thing I wasn't a complete dunce at. At the time, it was just easier to give in, and, to be fair, I'm glad I did it. I like cooking, and I can earn my living, but. . .'

'But you wanted to study archaeology?'

She nodded. 'I know it's not a very sensible idea. I did mention it tentatively, but my parents produced all sorts of reasons for not trying: I wouldn't get on the course, I wouldn't be able to cope, and if I did I'd never get a decent job at the end of it all.' She looked at Lefteris at last. 'It's different for you. You're strong. You'd never let anyone bully you, but I haven't got the confidence. I just cave in.'

'That doesn't sound like the spitfire who burst into my office and gave me a piece of her mind after Discovery Crete collapsed,' he commented, and she looked away again.

'It's different here,' she said in a burst of honesty. 'It's one of the reasons I don't want to go home. I feel different here, and you're different from my parents too.' She folded one of the paper napkins into a concertina. 'You make my angry,' she added in a low voice, 'but you don't make me feel useless.'

'I'm glad to hear it.' He was looking strangely grim, but it didn't seem to be directed at her. 'Presumably your parents didn't approve of your coming to Crete?'

'No, they were horrified. They thought I was mad to throw up my job at the wine bar for a silly whim, and when I insisted they washed their hands of me all together.'

'What made you stand up to them this time?'

'My parents entertain a lot. Their dinner parties are awful. Everyone's so confident about their opinions, and if anyone remembers to ask me mine I go all tongue-tied and pathetic, and as soon as I do manage to say something they all jump down my throat and ask me to justify myself.' Courtney shuddered. 'I hate it! My parents ask along "suitable" young men for me — they think the best they can do for me now is to marry me off — but they only come in the hope that they'll see Ginny. I can see them wondering how on earth she manages to have such a dull, dowdy sister.'

A smile flickered across Lefteris's face. 'They wouldn't think that if they had seen you taking off your clothes without a thought as to who might be watching!'

Courtney flushed and bit her lip. 'I would never have done that if I'd known you were there!'

'No,' he said slowly. 'I believe you wouldn't.'

Across the table, their eyes met and for Courtney it was as if a hand were squeezing all the air out of her lungs. Tearing her eyes away, she took a sharp breath to steady her pulse. 'Anyway,' she went on, trying to sound brisk, 'a couple of months ago, they had a cocktail party, and one of the guests was a historian who does a lot of television documentaries. I thought he'd be ghastly, but he was charming. He had a way of making you tell him things you never meant to tell him at all.' A bit like Lefteris himself, she added mentally. 'He found out how interested I was in the Minoans, and he told me about the course. He was the one who suggested that I come to Crete so that when I applied I could prove that I'd made a real effort to do as much as I could by myself. He said that you should always follow your instincts and do what you really want to do, even if it doesn't seem sensible or practical at the time.' Her smile glimmered in the dim light. 'So here I am.'

'Yes,' said Lefteris thoughtfully. 'Here you are.'

Without knowing why, Courtney's heartbeat slowed to an erratic, painful thud. She swallowed, not daring to meet his eyes, and was ridiculously relieved to find the proprietor hovering over them, presenting two tiny glasses of raki on the house as he distracted Lefteris with small talk.

Courtney gulped at the fiery liquid, coughing as the spirit burned down her throat and hoping that it would drown the treacherous desire uncurling within her. She wanted to touch him, to lay her hand against his cheek and press her lips to the pulse in his throat. She wanted to run her fingers through his dark hair and feel his hard body beneath her hands.

She must stop this! As if from a great distance, she saw him rise and shake hands with the proprietor before turning to pull out her chair. Her smile felt stiff as she stood up and her pulse roared so loudly in her ears that she had no idea what he was saying. She supposed she must have said something suitable, for the next minute they were outside. The night air was cool on her bare skin, but her knees felt stupidly weak as they walked along the quayside. The moonlight etched the distinctive line of his nose and jaw, and touched the corner of his mouth. Lucky moonlight, she thought and shivered with pure desire.

'Are you cold?'

'What?' she asked stupidly.

'You shivered,' he said in amusement. 'I wondered if you were cold.'

Her mouth felt dry. 'A bit.'

'Here, have my jacket.' He unslung his jacket and draped it round her shoulders. Courtney stood very still, wondering if he could hear the slow, reverberating boom, boom, boom of her heart. For a long moment, he just stood there, looking down at her.

'What's the matter?' she said, when she could bear the silence no longer.

He didn't answer immediately. Reaching out, he eased her tumbled hair over the collar and smoothed down one of the lapels. 'I was just remembering that you were English,' he said at last.

'Yes, I am.' His nearness was mesmerising and she stared woodenly at his tie, unable to meet his eyes. 'But I'm not like Sabrina or Linda.'

Very gently, he ran his finger down her soft cheek, the barest of caresses. 'I'm beginning to think that you might not be,' he agreed.

Courtney could feel her cheek burning from that brief touch as they drove home. The clouds had rolled down from the mountains, and the darkness seemed very close. Normally the view was wide, rolling grandly up to the peaks, but now everything was in flashes of close-ups as the headlights sliced through the night: fruit hanging heavy on the orange trees, a clump of leggy lavender clinging to the rocks at a bend in the road, the spear-shaped elegance of an Italian cypress.

She sat stiffly in her seat, staring straight ahead, terrified that if she so much as brushed against Lefteris she would simply burst into flames. When he stopped the car outside the high stone wall and switched off the engine, the silence was absolute. Courtney found that it took all her effort to concentrate on breathing, and her body felt jerky and uncoordinated as she carried the shopping bags up to the kitchen.

He brought most of them, but much to her relief he left her to put the groceries away by herself. It was easier to breathe when he had gone. Courtney emptied the fruit into huge baskets and stacked the vegetables in the fridge. She had come so close to making a monumental fool of herself! She lingered as long as she could in the kitchen, until she had herself under better control.

Tempted to go straight to bed, she hesitated when

she saw that the lights were still on and the door open on to the terrace. She could hardly sneak off, not when he had taken her out to dinner. Taking a deep breath, she walked over to the door. She would wish him a goodnight from there, and then go. What harm was there in that?

Lefteris was standing on the terrace, looking out to the mountains, a glass in his hand. He turned as if he sensed her hesitating in the doorway. 'Come over here,' he said.

And, like a fool, she went.

'Look at this.' He gestured with his glass, and Courtney drew a long breath. The clouds, still thick overhead, had drifted on, leaving a narrow swath of clear sky over the mountain-tops. The snow on the peaks shone eerily white and serene in the moonlight, seeming to float disembodied over the dark valley.

'Oh,' was all she said, but it seemed to be enough.

He put down his glass on the wall. The chink of glass against stone was abnormally loud in the stillness. Courtney reacted as if to a shot.

'I just came to say goodnight,' she said hurriedly, and would have stepped back if he hadn't reached out and taken hold of her bare arms. His hands seared into her skin.

'I've been thinking about what your friend the historian said,' he said, drawing her irresistibly towards him.

'What about?' Her voice was a cracked, humiliating whisper.

'About following your instincts, even when it doesn't seem sensible.' He slid his hands up her arms and let them drift beneath the tumble of silky hair to cup her neck. 'I thought it might be interesting to test his theory,' he said tilting up her face.

Courtney quivered, helpless against the desire that beat at her. Taking a shuddering breath, she opened her mouth to speak. She never knew what she would

have said, but by then it was too late anyway. Lefteris
had bent his head and captured her lips with his own,
and the fire which had been simmering relentlessly
inside her exploded into a terrifying blaze of feeling
where nothing existed beyond the touch of his mouth
and the feel of his body.

It was what she had hungered for all evening.
Courtney melted against his granite strength, murmuring deep in her throat, half in pleasure, half in protest
at her own weakness as she gave in and let her arms
slide around him.

'Glykia mou,' he murmured into her ear, disentangling his fingers from her hair to pull her hard
against him, his kiss deeper and more insistent. More
dangerous, more exciting.

Her hands spread over his back, feeling his warmth
through the thin material of his shirt, abandoning
herself to the wicked thrill of his mouth exploring hers,
of hers exploring his, of his hands, hard and insistent
on her body.

When he released her, she couldn't prevent a small
moan of protest. Dazed and disorientated by the
sensations still swirling through her, she could only
stare up at him.

'That definitely wasn't very sensible.' The edge of
rueful amusement in his voice helped Courtney pull
herself together more effectively than a slap in the
face.

'Perhaps the theory doesn't work after all,' she said
unevenly, trying desperately to straighten her trembling legs.

'I don't know about that,' he said. His face was
inscrutable in the darkness. 'I think your friend was
right. Kissing you might not have been sensible, but it
was certainly worth it.'

The next day, Courtney wondered if she had dreamt
that devastating kiss. She had lain awake all night,

burning with a dreadful combination of humiliation and unsatisfied desire, wondering how on earth she would be able to face him in the morning, but in the event she needn't have worried. She only saw Lefteris briefly, when he behaved as if absolutely nothing had happened.

'I'm off to the airport to meet the plane,' he said, coming into the kitchen where she was chopping onions. 'I've arranged for the other cars and drivers to meet at the airport, so we'll all come back together. Is everything ready for lunch when we get back?'

'It will be,' Courtney said shortly, resenting his ability to behave as if he had never held her in his arms, or kissed her to a fever pitch of desire. Still, if he wanted to pretend it had never happened, that was fine by her!

It was a cosmopolitan group that sat down to lunch that first day. Directors of divisions in Belgium, Portugal, the Netherlands and Spain were there with their wives, as well as the Italian director, Gianni Neri, whose wife was apparently ill, and Inger, who was tall and blonde and Danish, with stunning Nordic blue eyes. Inger, Courtney learnt, was head of Lefteris's PR organisation, and if she had a husband there was no sign of him. Lefteris drove Inger up in his car, letting the others follow behind, and Courtney loathed her on sight.

At least lunch was a success, and all the guests — with the notable exception of Inger, who was too busy keeping Lefteris riveted to her side — were flatteringly appreciative. Lefteris did manage to tear himself away from what was no doubt a fascinating discussion about PR to introduce Courtney when she brought in the coffee, but she took the first opportunity to escape back to the kitchen. The company was too sophisticated for her, too assured, all too reminiscent of those endless dinner parties at home, and she retreated instinctively into a shy gawkiness that her parents would have recognised only too well.

It was a very long week. The guests spent their time sitting around the pool or on the terrace, recovering from the endless meals that Courtney produced. Lefteris was a good host, ensuring that his guests enjoyed themselves without ever once pressurising them into anything they didn't want to do, but at the same time there was no doubt who was boss. The directors all treated him with deference and although Courtney never once saw him pull rank there was a distinctive aura of power about him that set him apart from the rest and was as indefinable as it was unmistakable

In the mornings, the directors would disappear to discuss business, and with Lefteris and Inger out of the way Courtney would perch on the wall and chat to the wives, who turned out to be much friendlier and less intimidating than her first impression. It was from them she learnt more about Lefteris. Generally, it seemed, they respected him as the head of a huge multinational concern — far larger and more powerful than Courtney had guessed — but they were greatly in awe of him.

'He's so different here, though,' said Consuelo, the Spanish director's wife. 'His city apartments are very luxurious, and immaculately run by his servants, but somehow they're not as welcoming as here. It's as if Lefteris uses them, but does not *live* there. He's always on the move. He works tremendously long hours when he's travelling, but when he's here he relaxes. It seems to be the only place he feels at home.' She glanced at Courtney. 'I think it would be different if he had a wife. She would be someone to go home to in the evenings.'

Courtney was longing to know more about Inger, but no one seemed to know very much about her. There had been rumours linking her with Lefteris, they admitted, but no one had ever known for sure. Inger, it appeared, never wasted her time talking to the wives. She was only interested in her career — and Lefteris, Courtney added to herself. Whenever she saw them together, the Danish girl had her hand on his arm, or her gleaming blonde head bent towards his dark one. They seemed to spend an awful lot of time out on the terrace too. Surely no one could talk about PR for that long?

Unable to bear the sight of them together, Courtney did her best to avoid him. Occasionally, he suggested that she join them for coffee, or come out for a swim, but she would haughtily refuse, claiming that she had things to do in the kitchen, and after a while he stopped asking. Inger always viewed her exit with satisfaction. Several times Courtney caught the other woman watching her with cold blue eyes, and knew with sure feminine instinct that for some reason the Danish girl disliked her intensely.

The understanding she and Lefteris had reached in Hania had vanished, and sometimes Courtney wondered if it had ever been there at all. She could hardly recognise the man who had sat across the table and listened to her babbling on about how inadequate she had always felt. Was this autocratic, cosmopolitan tycoon who inspired such awe in his directors the same man who had sat on the roof at Knossos and told her the story of Theseus and the Labyrinth? The same man who had carried her shopping and walked through the back streets of Hania? The man who had kissed her? Whenever Courtney thought about that kiss, she shook with a gust of shame and longing — and fury with herself for caring so much. Why had he bothered to kiss her at all when he knew that Inger, perfect un-English Inger, would be arriving the very next day?

After lunch, everyone would retire for a siesta. Lefteris went to his room, she knew, and she imagined that the others did the same. She would go for a walk instead, knowing that if she lay down she would just end up remembering Lefteris and the feel of his body.

One afternoon, she was just finishing clearing the kitchen after lunch when the door opened and Inger appeared. Courtney eyed her enviously. She was so svelte and well-groomed, always dressed with that casual, unstudied style that inevitably made Courtney feel a frump.

'Can I get you something?' She had to force herself to sound polite.

For once, Inger seemed determined to be friendly. 'I wondered if I could have a bottle of champagne? And two glasses?' She fluttered her lashes, girlishly confiding, 'It's for a little surprise.'

No guesses as to who the other glass was for, or what the surprise was! 'Celebrating?' Courtney asked, pinning a smile to her lips.

Inger gave a small, secret smile. 'Just the pleasure of a couple of hours alone together.' Her frosty blue eyes met Courtney's. 'You know how it is.'

'Of course,' said Courtney woodenly. So this was what Lefteris did in his siesta! She tried reminding herself that it was no business of hers but it didn't stop the bitter jealousy clawing at her heart.

Inger watched as as she fetched the champagne, filled the ice bucket and produced two glasses. The Danish girl was the only guest who made her feel like a servant, and her only thanks was a small, insincere smile as she gathered up the bottle and swayed off in the direction of Lefteris's room.

Courtney found that her hands were shaking as she let herself out of the kitchen and escaped out into the olive groves. The dappled silence was soothing, and the long, feathery grass tickled her legs as they swayed silver-white in the breeze. Leaning back against a gnarled trunk, she closed her eyes, and breathed in the sweet smell of clover. She could hear bees zooming among the flowers which blurred the grass with colour, and the distant clank of a sheep's bell.

None of it could shut out the thought of Inger and Lefteris, sharing the champagne, laughing, making love. Courtney had glimpsed inside his room once. It was simply, even starkly furnished with a huge, half-canopied iron bed, a scrubbed wooden floor and heavily carved chests. The shutters had been open, and the room was full of sunlight.

Was he there now, with the shutters closed against the heat? Was he lying on that wide bed? Was Inger with him?

Courtney's eyes flew open, the pain blocking her throat and tightening its grip around her heart so viciously that for a moment she couldn't breathe. Jumping to her feet, she pressed the heels of her hands against her eyes. She *wouldn't* cry. There was absolutely nothing to cry about. All she had to do was get through three more days, and then she would be free to go. She tried to imagine where she would be in a week's time, but her mind obstinately refused to move beyond Agios Giorgios and Lefteris.

Walking slowly back along the narrow track that led between the olive groves, she met Gianni Neri, head bent and hands thrust into his trouser pockets. He looked as miserable as she felt, and she summoned a smile to greet him. He was an attractive man of about forty with a warm Italian smile, and he had been particularly nice to her since he had arrived, always ready with compliments on her cooking.

Gianni's greeting was as forced as her own. 'Is something wrong?' she asked impulsively as he turned to walk back with her.

He sighed. 'I'm sorry, I'm not very good company, am I? That's why I came out for a walk. It's a strain pretending to have a good time when I can't stop thinking about my problems.'

'I know what it's like,' said Courtney quietly. Her

own unhappiness made her more sensitive to his. 'Is there anything I can do to help?'

'Not really.' Gianni walked in silence for a few moments, staring down at the camomile that grew in the middle of the track.

'It's my wife, Paola,' he burst out at last. 'I told Lefteris that she wasn't well, but she's fine. She just refused to come.' He bit his lip. 'You'd think that anyone would be delighted to spend a week in a place like this, wouldn't you?'

'I suppose it depends what you're used to,' Courtney said awkwardly.

'She said she was fed up with travelling and wanted to stay in Rome. We had a terrible row just before I left for Athens, and I haven't been able to speak to her since.' He sighed again and raked his hands through his hair. 'I have to travel. It's part of my job as head of the Italian division and I can't just throw it all in. Quite apart from anything else, it's what keeps her in all the luxury she could ever want, but she doesn't seem to understand that. We haven't been married very long. She's much younger than me, too, and she's very beautiful. . .' Gianni trailed off hopelessly. 'I'm sorry, I didn't mean to burden you with all this.'

He was obviously worried about what his young and beautiful wife was up to without him, especially after a major argument. Courtney didn't blame him.

'Perhaps she just needs time to adjust to the fact that your job is important to you,' she suggested.

Gianni looked doubtful. 'I hope so. It would help if she was better at entertaining, but she doesn't like cooking and says just the thought of producing an elaborate meal makes her go to pieces.'

'I can understand that.'

'You? You cook like an angel!'

Courtney smiled at the extravagant compliment. 'Cooking is the only thing I *can* do, though. I'm happy in the kitchen, but I'd go to pieces too at the thought of presiding over a grand dinner party. I'm hopeless at anything like that. I never know what to say to anyone.'

'I would never have guessed,' said Gianni with a curious look. 'We have all thought you charming. In fact, some of us wondered whether there might be something between you and Lefteris.' He spread his hands apologetically at Courtney's horrified expression. 'It was just something in the way he looked at you whenever you came into the room,' he explained.

'There's nothing between us,' she said with unnecessary emphasis. 'Nothing at all. I'm just his cook — and a temporary one, at that.'

'Yes, that's what Lefteris said, too,' Gianni hastened to reassure her. 'I overheard Inger teasing him about it. I wouldn't dare,' he said frankly, 'but a few years ago there were some rumours going round about Lefteris and Inger, so perhaps she feels she can ask. Anyway, he just said coolly that you were just a cook who had conveniently been able to take over from Katina for a while.'

Just a cook. Courtney's smile was brittle. 'That's right.' Why was she so surprised? She had known all along what she meant to him: just a cook. Why would he need anything else when he had Inger with her long legs and her blue eyes and her surprise bottles of champagne?

'How long will you be working for him?' Gianni asked suddenly.

'Just as long as you're all here. Katina should be back soon.' Even if she wasn't, Courtney intended to leave as soon as she could. She wasn't going to hang around as *just a cook*, however convenient it was for Lefteris!

'Will you stay in Crete?'

'For a couple of weeks.' She forced her mind back to what Gianni was asking. 'I'll probably go over to the east and explore some of the Minoan sites.' Courtney wished she sounded more enthusiastic at the prospect.

'And then what?' he persisted.

She was silent. She would have to think about it some time. 'I don't really know,' she said feebly.

Gianni took her arm and stopped her. 'Would you consider a job in Rome?'

'Rome?'

'You could be our cook,' he said eagerly. 'I'm sure that if Paola didn't have to worry about the food she would feel less nervous about entertaining. I don't know why I didn't think of it before! We could agree a salary, whatever you wanted, and there's a self-contained flat you could have,' he rushed on. 'I'm sure you would get on with Paola. People think she should be confident because she's so pretty, but really she's very shy, and you would probably understand that.'

'I don't know,' Courtney said slowly. 'I hadn't thought about going somewhere like Rome.'

'But you'll think about it, at least?' Gianni pleaded as they reached the gate.

What were her alternatives? A job at home, a job abroad; at the moment every idea that didn't involve staying in Agios Giorgios seemed equally flat, but she would have to do something.

'Yes, I'll think about it.'

Gianni beamed. 'Good.' He held open the gate for her and they began walking up the steps. 'And thank you for listening, Courtney. I feel better for having talked to someone.'

'I'm glad,' she said simply. She put her hand on his arm, wanting to encourage him. 'Perhaps being on her own for a week will give Paola a chance to think things through as well. She'll probably be so pleased to see you when you get back that she'll be willing to tackle a dozen dinner parties!'

'I hope so,' said Gianni. He covered her hand with

his own and looked down at her with warm brown eyes. 'Thank you!' he said seriously.

At that moment, Lefteris came down the steps looking thunderous. 'Am I interrupting something?' he asked coldly as Courtney snatched her hand from under Gianni's with a ridiculously guilty start.

'Of course not,' said Gianni easily enough, but his cheekbones were tinged with colour. Courtney guessed that he wouldn't want his formidable boss to know that he had been pouring out his personal problems to Lefteris's cook. 'I was just telling Courtney how much we've all been enjoying her cooking.'

'I'm sure she appreciates your compliments,' Lefteris said with such a snap that Gianni cast him a puzzled look, murmured an excuse and hurried away up the steps. Courtney would have followed him, but Lefteris grabbed her arm in an iron grip and pulled her back.

'Where have you been?' he demanded furiously.

Courtney shook herself free of his hand. 'For a walk,' she said tightly.

'With Gianni?'

'For part of the way, yes. Have you any objections?'

A muscle beat in his jaw. 'You're supposed to be here as a cook.'

'I presumed I was allowed five minutes off every now and then,' she retorted sarcastically. 'I didn't realise I had to ask permission every time I stepped out of the kitchen!'

'Of course you're allowed time off,' he scowled. 'I'd rather you didn't spend it flirting with my guests, that's all.'

'I have not been flirting!' said Courtney, outraged. 'I happened to meet Signor Neri on my way back from my walk. What was I supposed to do? Walk past and refuse to talk to him? You ought to be glad I'm prepared to be pleasant to your guests.'

'There's a difference between being pleasant and allowing yourself to be pawed,' he snarled. 'I noticed you weren't exactly pushing him away. What were you talking about so intensely together?'

Courtney sucked in her breath, as angry as he was now. 'That,' she said through her teeth, 'is none of your business!'

'At least you're not asking me to believe you spent all that time demurely listening to compliments about your cooking!'

'All *what* time?'

'You left at least an hour ago,' he pointed out in a harsh voice.

'I didn't realise you were keeping such a close eye on my movements,' Courtney said furiously. 'I thought you had better things to do this afternoon!' He probably had a hangover from all that champagne. Serve him right! 'Next time I'll make sure I clock in and out so that you can keep an exact account of how much time I take away from the kitchen! After all, we don't want to forget that I'm *just a cook* here, do we?' she added unable to keep the bitterness from her voice.

They glared at each other, the air between them crackling with tension. Courtney's eyes were bright with anger as she faced him out defiantly.

Lefteris let out a sharp breath of exasperation. 'Was Gianni with you all that time?'

'I can't see that it's got anything to do with you, but no, he wasn't. We walked down the track together for about ten minutes, hardly long enough to conduct an intense affair, even to your suspicious mind!' she said acidly. 'And now, if you've quite finished your interrogation, I'll get back to the kitchen where you seem so anxious to keep me!'

CHAPTER SEVEN

HEAD held high, Courtney stalked up the steps and slammed around the kitchen as she began the preparations for dinner. He had no right to cross-question her like that! What did he think she was, some kind of slave? Inger was welcome to him!

In a way, she was grateful for the anger that buoyed her up over the last few days. She was icily formal with Lefteris, but made a point of being charming to everybody else, with the exception of Inger, who ignored her, which was fine by Courtney. She was too bad-tempered to notice that Inger herself was looking tight-faced. Lefteris continued to look ominously grim, and glowered if he found her anywhere near Gianni, while Courtney wondered crossly what he expected her to do to him in full view of everybody else.

All in all, it was a relief when the last day arrived, and they all gathered on the terrace before being driven down to the airport. Courtney was touched by the effusive compliments on her cooking as they all said goodbye to her, and Gianni wrung her hand. 'Remember what we talked about,' he said, producing a business card out of his jacket pocket. 'Here is my telephone number. Call me if you ever change your mind.'

Over his shoulder, Courtney caught sight of Lefteris lurking with a black expression. 'Thanks, Gianni,' she said with a bright smile and a challenging look at Lefteris. 'I may just do that.'

Lefteris's glare was all she hoped it would be.

When they had all gone, Courtney was left alone to collapse on to the wooden bench. Lefteris had gone to see his guests off at the airport, but he would be back,

113

and if that last look he had given her was anything to go by he would be in a filthy temper.

Irritated with herself for being so nervous, she got up with a sigh. In spite of what he thought about her time off, she had been cooking intensively all week, and she was tired. The kitchen had been thoroughly cleaned in preparation for Katina's return, and all she had to do was pack.

Folding her clothes into the case with unnatural concentration, Courtney tried not to think about the fact that she would ever again wake in this lovely bright room with the sunshine streaming through the shutters, never lie in the dark as the fragrance of the jasmine outside drifted on the night air. It was the last time she would walk across the cool hall or down the steps to the wooden gate. It was the last time she would see Lefteris.

Half of her was tempted to leave without having to face him again, but a sterner side warned her that it would be stupid, as well as rude. She hadn't been paid yet. And anyway, what was there to worry about? She had done a good job, had kept her part of the bargain. It wasn't her fault if he was in a bad mood because Inger wouldn't be interrupting his siesta with any more surprise bottles of champagne.

She dropped her case on the terrace and told herself all the reasons why she would be glad not to see him again. He was arrogant, selfish, domineering, completely unreasonable. He was pigheaded and so eaten up with pride he couldn't see what was in front of his own nose. He had spent the entire week drooling over Inger and had had the cheek to accuse her of encouraging Gianni just because she had been offering him a little sympathy. He was a chauvinist. He was narrow-minded. He was absolutely hateful, in fact.

By the time he returned, she had talked herself into a truculent mood which was only exacerbated when his black brows drew together in a menacing frown as he caught sight of her sitting next to her suitcase on the terrace.

'What do you think you're doing?'

'Waiting to be paid,' she said shortly. 'Was I expected to wait in the kitchen?'

His mouth was set in an angry line. 'You seem very anxious to leave, Courtney. Nothing to do with the fact that your friend Gianni has gone? No more secret smiles or whispering on the terrace? No more romantic strolls through the olive groves?'

'I'm leaving because my job is finished,' she said stonily.

He strode over to the terrace wall and stood glowering out at the White Mountains, his back rigid with hostility. 'He's married, you know,' he burst out at last.

'I know he's married,' Courtney said, her jaw clenched with the effort of not losing her temper. 'He told me all about his wife.'

'Oh, very cosy,' sneered Lefteris, swinging round to face her once more. 'I suppose she doesn't understand him! Don't tell me you fell for that old line?'

Courtney was white with suppressed fury. 'There wasn't any *line*. Gianni spoke to me in confidence, and I've got no intention of repeating what he said, especially not to *you*! I was just someone for him to talk to.'

'Really?' he said sarcastically. 'It didn't look that way to me!'

'Frankly, I'm surprised you even noticed Gianni was there at all,' Courtney flared, jumping to her feet as she lost the battle with her temper. 'You had more than enough on your hands with all your secret, surprise meetings with Inger. How you can accuse Gianni of flirting when you barely took your hands off her all week beats me!'

'Inger is a respected colleague, that's all,' he said furiously.

'Really?' she mimicked his tone exactly. 'It didn't look that way to me!'

'*Yia onoma tou Theou*!' Lefteris swore and for a moment Courtney thought he was going to hit her. His jaw worked convulsively. 'What are you going to do now?' he asked harshly when he had himself under better control.

'How can I decide until I've been paid?'

'Oh, very well!' He strode into his study and reappeared a few moments later to drop a bundle of notes contemptuously at her feet. 'I might have known that all you'd be interested in was money. Linda wouldn't leave until she'd been paid either!'

There was an angry pause. Hating him, Courtney stooped to pick up the notes and stuff them into her bag. He was the one who had offered her the job, after all! Did he expect her to slave away in his kitchen all week just for the joy of being near him?

He paced over to the wall once more. 'So, where will you go first?' he asked as if the words were dragged out of him.

'Hania then Heraklion, I suppose. I haven't really thought about it.'

'And after that?'

'I don't know. I'll have to get a job.'

'In Rome?'

'Why not?' She met his gaze squarely, her eyes bright with fury. 'I may as well make the most of my opportunities.'

'Oh, you've done that all right! You've had as much as you can out of me, so you've decided to go to work on Gianni with those big eyes of yours! I, of all people, should have known what to expect from an English girl, but, like a fool, I actually believed all that sanctimonious hypocrisy about fighting to be independent and wanting to study. We haven't heard much about *that* since Gianni started escorting you out to the olive groves! I suppose you've told him that you've always wanted to study the Ancient Romans? It didn't take much to persuade you that the bright lights and another gullible man might be an easier option. If I had any fellow feeling, I'd warn Gianni about what he's taking on, but he deserves everything that's coming his way! "Call me if you ever change your mind." It's not hard to guess what kind of offer *that* was!'

Courtney had never been so angry. 'It's not hard to guess what kind of offers you were making Inger either, but I'm not carrying on as if it's any of my business! You can do what you like with her as far as I'm concerned.'

'I don't need my cook's permission to do anything,' Lefteris snarled.

'I'm not your cook any more,' she reminded him savagely, picking up her case. 'That means *I* don't have to stay here and listen to you being your usual pig-headed, arrogant, loathsome self any longer'

'Don't be childish,' he said unfairly. 'You can't walk out at this time of night!'

'Oh, can't I? Watch me!' Courtney headed for the steps, boiling with such rage that she hardly noticed the weight of her case.

'You won't get to Hania tonight,' he shouted, following her to the top of the steps and watching her reach for the gate. 'You'll come crawling back here in an hour because you haven't got anywhere to sleep!'

Courtney had the gate open now. She turned to look up at him, tight-faced and stormy-eyed. 'Quite frankly,' she said distinctly, 'I'd rather sleep with Dimitra's goat than ever set foot here again!' And she banged the gate shut behind her.

Sheer fury carried her down the track, but when she reached the road she stopped for breath. Putting down her case, she rubbed her arm. It didn't sound as if he was coming after her. He didn't care that much what happened to her, obviously! Not that she cared, she reminded herself bitterly. He probably just wanted her to stay and cook his dinners until Katina came back. Well, it wouldn't do him any harm to learn how to tell one saucepan from another, and if he couldn't do that, let him starve!

She picked up her case and began to trudge more slowly down the road. Where *was* she going to spend the night? It had been very satisfying slamming the door behind her, but a small voice inside her pointed out that it hadn't been all that sensible. Lefteris's taunt about crawling back to the villa echoed in her head and she lifted her chin. There was no way she was going to give him *that* satisfaction!

She was almost at the village when she heard a car behind her. Lefteris? Her heart leapt. The case was very heavy now, but she refused to put it down and look as if she was waiting for him. Determinedly not looking round, she plodded on. If he thought she would throw herself into his arms after all those vile things he had said to her, he had another think coming!

The car slowed. Courtney stuck her nose in the air and stepped ostentatiously on to the verge without stopping, and the car passed her, only to pull up a little further on. It was an open-topped Mercedes, but Courtney only registered that it wasn't Lefteris. She was furious with herself for being so bitterly disappointed.

'Courtney?' It was Nikos.

Courtney put her case down uncertainly. She hadn't seen Nikos since she had stormed back to accuse Lefteris of bankrupting Discovery Crete, and it took her a few moments to register who he was.

'Is something wrong?' he asked in concern. 'Where are you going with your case at this time of night?'

'Hania,' said Courtney stiffly.

'But I thought you were working for Lefteris Markakis?'

'I was.' Her eyes snapped with remembered fury,

fuelled anew by the bitterness of knowing that he hadn't bothered to come after her. 'Not any more!'

Nikos eyed her thoughtfully. 'It's getting late. Wouldn't you be better to leave tomorrow?'

'I'm not going back to the villa,' Courtney said through her teeth.

A look that might have been satisfaction flickered across Nikos's face. 'Well, I can't leave you here, not with that heavy case. Let me give you a lift.'

She hesitated. Lefteris had made Nikos sound evil and treacherous, but it was only his word against Nikos's after all, and why should she believe everything *he* had said? Courtney glanced at Nikos. She had forgotten how good-looking he was, and when he smiled so charmingly at her it was impossible to imagine that he had set up Discovery Crete simply as a way of humiliating Lefteris. There must be some other reason why Lefteris hated him so much. . .

She glanced over her shoulder, but there was no sign of him. He obviously couldn't be bothered to follow her. She looked back at Nikos and his gleaming car. Something deep inside her told her to refuse, but what option did she have? She couldn't stand out here all night, and, if Lefteris didn't care what happened to her, why *shouldn't* she accept a lift from Nikos? It wasn't Nikos who had thrown her out of a job just to ensure that he got his own way. Nikos hadn't done anything to her. *He* hadn't been utterly unreasonable, or let her storm off without making the slightest attempt to stop her. If Lefteris wouldn't like her accepting a lift from his enemy, so much the better!

'If it's not too much trouble. . .'

'No trouble at all,' he said promptly. 'It's the least I can do.' He lifted her suitcase into the back seat and held open the front door for her.

'How did you know I was working for Lefteris?' Courtney asked as she got in.

Nikos shut the door behind her and got into the

driver's seat to start the engine. 'You'd be surprised how quickly news gets round these small villages. To tell you the truth, I've been feeling rather guilty about you, so I'm glad of a chance to help.'

'Guilty? About me?'

'I'm afraid I wasn't thinking very clearly when you came to see me that day. I'd only just heard about the bankruptcy myself, and was still rather shocked. Later, I was going to offer you somewhere to stay until we found out exactly what was happening, but then I heard you were staying with Markakis.' Nikos shrugged. 'I don't blame you. It's a very pleasant place to stay, and I didn't think any offers from me would be particularly welcomed, particularly as I imagine he lost no opportunity to blacken my name.'

'He doesn't seem to like you very much,' Courtney admitted. Her blind rage had subsided somewhat by now, and she felt rather uncomfortable discussing Lefteris with Nikos.

'Did he tell you why?'

'I gathered there was some kind of vendetta between your families.'

'That's true, but there's more to it than that,' said Nikos. 'Did he tell you about Linda?'

'His brother's wife?' said Courtney cautiously. 'He mentioned that they hadn't been very happily married.'

'Lefteris likes to think they weren't happy, but it's not true,' said Nikos. 'Linda was devoted to Christos, but his family hated the idea of his marrying her. Lefteris was practically engaged to an English girl once, but she couldn't bear his arrogance, and she left him eventually for another man. You can imagine what that did to a man of Lefteris's pride! He never got over the humiliation, and when Christos brought Linda to Crete he and the rest of his family did everything they could to make her feel unwelcome just because she was English. Lefteris kept Christos's nose to the grindstone so that he had no time to devote to his bride, and she was desperately lonely. I met her in Hania one day. I think I was the only friend she had here, and it was me she ran to when Christos died.'

Courtney stared down at her hands, listening but saying nothing. It was more or less the same story Lefteris had told her, but seen from a different perspective. Which version was the true one?

'Christos was killed in a car crash a few months after they were married,' Nikos went on. 'It was a tragic accident, but you'd think it was all Linda's fault the way his family carried on. She was distraught, of course, and all she wanted was to go home, but she didn't get a penny from that family, and you know how rich they are!' Nikos's voice was tinged with bitter envy. 'Lefteris wouldn't even notice if he lost a few million, but he wasn't going to give Linda anything. Everything was very cleverly tied up, and in the end all she had was Villa Athina, which Lefteris had given to her and Christos as an outright gift. Even he couldn't take that back! I offered to buy it off her just to give her some ready cash so that she could go home.'

'Is that why he hates you so much? Because you helped a friend?

'For him, it was a question of family honour,' said Nikos. 'He never forgave Linda for running to me for help, or me for helping her. Everyone knew where she was, and that the Markakis family hadn't helped one of its own. Lefteris hated that, even though it was true.'

Courtney found it hard to believe that Lefteris could be quite that vindictive, but she knew only too well how much he despised English girls. He had misjudged her just because she was English. Had he been wrong about Linda too?

She sat silently, wrapped in her thoughts until she suddenly noticed that Nikos had swung the car off the road to Hania and up towards his village. She sat bolt upright in her seat, stirred by a vague sense of unease. 'Where are we going?'

'It's quite a long drive into Hania,' Nikos said reasonably. 'You look too tired for the hassle of finding somewhere to stay at this time of night. Wouldn't you rather come and stay with us? My mother lives with me, so there's no ulterior motive, I assure you! I just thought you might like a good night's sleep.'

What could she say? Courtney wished she had never accepted a lift from him now. The last thing she wanted was to have hospitality pressed upon her but she could hardly insist that he turn round and drive her all the way into Hania. And what did it matter, anyway? She was tired and miserable and didn't care where she slept as long as there was a bed and she could be alone. There was no point in wondering what would have happened if Lefteris had come to find her and take her home. He hadn't, and right now nothing else really mattered.

Courtney woke the next morning wondering why a cold hand of misery was clamped over her heart. Then, as her eyes focused, she remembered. This was Nikos's house. She had walked out on Lefteris in a rage, and now she would never see him again. The bitter fury of last night had subsided, leaving her numb and weary.

It was dark in the room. Opening the shutters, she could see the morning light pouring down on to the other side of the valley. Nikos's house faced west and it would be some time before the sun reached here. The gloom was oppressive, and she stared longingly down at Agios Giorgios, basking in the sunshine. She felt marooned up here, cut off from the happiness she had known over the last few weeks. Even when she had been hating Lefteris, she had succumbed to the exhilaration of his presence, which made everything more alive, more interesting. Up here, she just felt flat. Her gaze rested on the olive groves. She couldn't see the villa, but she knew it was there. The sun would be filtering through the vines on to the terrace and throwing shadows behind the cracked *pithoi* in the courtyard. And Lefteris would be there, with his fierce, proud face. Would he be missing her? Would he be wondering where she was?

Why had she left?

She would have had to leave anyway, Courtney reminded herself dully, turning from the window. He didn't want her around. She was English, to be despised and distrusted. He was probably on the phone to Inger even now, persuading her to come back so that they could be alone together. . . Sick at heart, she dressed and went to find Nikos. It would be easier once she had left the valley.

But when she asked him about buses to Hania, Nikos threw up his hands in protest. 'You can't go so soon!'

'I'd really like to get over to Heraklion as soon as possible,' Courtney said awkwardly.

'You must stay at least tonight,' he insisted. 'I don't want you to leave here thinking that we all treat strangers as badly as Lefteris does.' He waved an arm at stacks of plastic chairs on the enormous terrace. 'Tonight I will hold a *glendi*, a feast in your honour. I have invited the whole district to show you what real Cretan hospitality is.'

Courtney's heart sank. 'It's very kind of you, but——'

'No buts!' Nikos brushed aside her attempt to demur. 'You are my honoured guest. I insist!' He spoke jovially enough, but there was something in his eyes that made Courtney hesitate. Somehow she didn't think she was going to be allowed to refuse. How could she? Nikos was clearly going to a tremendous effort to offer her hospitality. Surely there was nothing in that to give her this uncomfortable feeling of suspicion?

The day dragged past. Nikos's mother was a small, colourless woman who seemed more than a little afraid

of her son, and although she smiled nervously at
Courtney she refused to let her help in the kitchen.
Courtney was left to hang around, feeling awkward
and out of place, wishing that she had never accepted
a lift from Nikos in the first place. He was sympathetic,
charming, attentive, but for some reason she couldn't
put her finger on he made her increasingly uneasy.
Once or twice she caught him looking at her with the
pleased, narrowed look of a hunter that had spotted its
prey, but the next moment he would be all smiles and
charm and she decided that she must have imagined it.
In the face of such relentless hospitality, her doubts
seemed ungracious and absurd.

Left to her own devices, she spent most of the day
wandering around. Higher than Agios Giorgios, the
village had an alpine air, and from a distance Nikos's
terrace looked more like a liner than ever, afloat on a
sea of pines and cypresses that dropped down the hill
towards the end of the gorge. The river course was dry
and bouldery, overhung by trees, and on the far side
was the aromatic scrub that she remembered so well,
sweeping round the valley to Agios Giorgios. She
turned her eyes resolutely away. Think about the
future, she told herself. Don't think about how Lefteris
looked the last time you saw him. Don't think about
his voice or his smile or the shivery excitement of his
touch.

Preparations for the party were in full swing when
she got back. Long trestle-tables had been laid out on
the terrace, and two lambs were already turning on a
spit. Courtney was dreading the evening ahead, but
there was nothing for it but to put a good face on it
and go and change. In the hope that it would make her
feel fetter, she put on a short-sleeved dress with an old-
fashioned print of bright pink flowers, but when she
looked in the mirror her face looked dull and drawn,
and her eyes an unhappy grey.

Nikos didn't seem to have been exaggerating when

he'd said that he had asked the whole district. When Courtney reluctantly made her appearance, the terrace was crowded with people, all talking and laughing. They were all strangers. Looking carefully, she couldn't recognise a single person from Agios Giorgios. She wondered whether Nikos had invited them, or whether they shared Lefteris's opinion of him and had deliberately stayed away.

She felt like a traitor just being there, and yet she couldn't really object to Nikos sticking close by her side like a good host. He made a point of introducing her to everyone, although the faces and names were just a blur after a while. Her Greek wasn't nearly good enough to follow what was said, but she heard Lefteris's name mentioned often, and she had an uncomfortable feeling of being on display.

It was the worst evening of Courtney's life. The party was wildly successful. The tables groaned with food, and the guests all ate and drank and thoroughly enjoyed themselves. Someone brought out a Cretan lyre, and someone else a lute, and there was singing and dancing, led by men who leapt and stamped and whirled in a fantastic display of energy. The noise was tremendous, and when volleys of gunfire started to go off below the terrace no one took the slightest notice.

'What's all that shooting?' Courtney asked Nikos, glancing nervously behind her.

'Oh, don't worry about the guns,' he said easily. 'That's just the young men working off their high spirits with blanks. It happens all the time. Haven't you noticed how every signpost in the mountains is riddled with bullet holes?' His face changed as he caught sight of someone over her shoulder, beckoning him into the house. 'Excuse me,' he said, and hurried inside.

Alone in the boisterous crowd, Courtney felt despair wash over her, loneliness and misery overwhelming her pride like a vast, engulfing tidal wave. Suddenly, she didn't care about Sabrina or Inger any more. She didn't care if Lefteris had behaved unfairly to Linda, or accused her unjustly of flirting with Gianni. All she cared about was that he wasn't there. She wanted to see him, to be able to reach out and touch him, a longing so intense that it racked her body with a physical ache and made it hard to breathe. She missed him. If only she hadn't stormed off like that. If only he were here. If only he loved her.

Unable to keep smiling any longer, she fled to her room. Not bothering to turn on the light, she stood with her back to the door, taking deep breaths in the darkness and willing herself not to cry. There was no point in denying it any longer. She was in love with Lefteris.

She never knew how long she stood there fighting tears, but eventually she moved away from the door and sat on the bed, staring numbly at the floor. Why had she let herself love him, when it was so obvious that he would never have any interest in her? She tried reciting all the qualities that had so irritated her about him, but it didn't make any difference. She still loved him.

And she would have to learn to live without him. Courtney stiffened her spine. She would begin tomorrow. She would go to Knossos and Phaestos and Kato Zakro and learn as much as she could about the Minoans, just as she had originally intended to do. She would pretend that the last few weeks had never been, and that desire still meant no more than wanting to study instead of a scorching flame that consumed her body with need. She would wrap herself in ancient history, and forget the Cretan who had made her care only for the present.

In the meantime, she realised with a sigh, it would be at least another hour before she could legitimately claim she was tired and escape to bed. Another hour and this would all be over.

The thought helped Courtney to her feet. Smoothing

down her dress, she steeled herself to face the party
with a smile again and opened the door very quietly.
She didn't want anyone to know that she had been
hiding in her room. There were raised voices coming
from the living-room and Courtney tiptoed down the
corridor, reluctant to get involved in a scene.

She heard a phone being slammed down, and then
Nikos's voice, barely recognisable with fury. 'Months
we've had this planned, and then the fools don't turn
up,' he snarled. 'What's the news from Tripoli?'

'Only that they'd try again on Tuesday night, at the
same bay past Agia Roumeli.'

To Courtney's surprise, it was an unmistakably
Cockney voice, which explained why Nikos was talking
in English. Hesitating in the shadows, she watched the
light through the open door, afraid that they would see
her if she slipped past. It didn't sound like the sort of
conversation they would want overheard.

'Tuesday?' Nikos repeated savagely. 'That's another
two nights I've got to stall the buyer. Why can't they
bring it in tomorrow night?'

'Same reason as tonight,' the Cockney said laconi-
cally. 'You know what the wind on the southern coast
is like. They wouldn't have been able to get near the
shore.' An edge of satisfaction crept into his voice. 'I
told you we should have used a bigger boat.'

'Exactly the kind of boat that gets noticed, in fact,'
snapped Nikos. 'Do you think we want the police
poking around our hold? They're checking anything at
all suspicious nowadays. No, the fishing boat is better.
There are lots of boats just like her along that coast;
no one will think of looking twice.'

At the mention of police, Courtney began to edge
backwards, suddenly frightened. This was definitely
not a conversation to be caught eavesdropping on!

Nikos had his frustration under control and was
quickly changing his plans. 'We'll still use the donkeys.
They're the best over that wild country, and no one

will ever know you've been there. You'd better go now and stop Andreas before he leaves for the pick-up tonight. Make sure he can do Tuesday night instead, and I'll meet you with the truck on the Imbros road. Andreas knows the place. Warn the others too.'

It was at that moment that Courtney, creeping cautiously back to her room, stumbled over a cat in the darkness and nearly died of fright at its blood-curdling yowl of protest.

'What was that?' Nikos asked sharply. 'See if there's anyone there.'

Courtney glanced wildly around, instinct telling her to run rather than stay and reason. They would soon find her in any of the rooms, but she would have to pass the door if she ran outside. The music and laughter on the terrace helped her make up her mind, and she bolted for the safety of numbers. As she fled past the door, she heard Nikos snap, 'The English girl! Get her back here!'

Her heart was thundering as she skidded out on to the terrace and plunged into the middle of a laughing group around the dancers. Surely he couldn't do anything to her here, in the middle of all these people, could he? *Could* he? Courtney's mind spun in frantic panic, remembering the menacing note in Nikos's voice. If he wanted her back, it wasn't just to ask if she was enjoying herself.

The feeling of having plunged into a nightmare was only intensified by the party continuing to whirl merrily around her. It was all too sudden, too unreal. She threw a fearful glance at the door. A very thin man with an unpleasantly battered face was standing next to Nikos, and the way they both searched the crowd with cold, professional eyes told her that this was no nightmare. Her danger was all too real. She shrank further behind the bulky figure of the woman next to her, but the stealthy movement must have attracted Nikos's eye. To her horror, she saw him tap the thin man's arm and point in her direction.

Courtney had never understood the term frozen with fear before, but she knew exactly what it meant now. She couldn't move, couldn't think. Her eyes swivelled helplessly around her. Even if she screamed, she couldn't speak Greek and explain, and it would be easy for Nikos to think up some reasonable excuse for taking her back into the house.

The thin man was making his way steadily through the crowds towards her. His lack of haste was more ominous than anything else. She would never be able to get away, but a surge of terrified adrenalin got Courtney moving again. She turned to run, but even as she did so a sudden stillness fell on the party. The lyre faltered and died as everyone turned towards the steps leading down from the terrace, and Courtney's reeling panic steadied miraculously.

Lefteris was standing there, dark and dangerous and infinitely reassuring. His face was grimly implacable, and the shotgun in his hands was pointing straight at Nikos's heart.

CHAPTER EIGHT

'WHERE is she?'

'I'm here!' Sobbing with relief, Courtney stumbled through the silent crowds towards him. 'I'm here! Please, please take me away!

Lefteris barely glanced at her. Everyone was very still, the gun in his hands rock-steady. Without raising his voice, he said something to Nikos in Greek, but the atmosphere was so tense that his words were very clear and a murmur of shock rippled through the crowd.

'Can we go?' pleaded Courtney, shivering at the murderous expression on Nikos's face.

Lefteris took one last look at Nikos, and then glanced slowly round at the crowd eyeing him with wary respect.

'Yes, we can go,' he said grimly. Taking her by the wrist, he practically dragged her down the steps to where his car was parked on the road. As they left, the party erupted into a babble of exclamation that didn't quite cover Nikos's snapped order to the Englishman, 'Don't let them get away!'

'They're coming after me,' she gasped, clinging to his hand.

'Not after——' Lefteris broke off with a smothered exclamation and ducked aside as a bullet whined past their ears and shattered his windscreen. Cursing, he pulled Courtney away from the car and down into the tangled darkness of the trees on the other side of the road. 'Those are real bullets!' he said incredulously as they crouched behind the cover of a thorn bush.

He peered round at his car. Nikos had run up to join the thin Englishman and they circled the car warily.

130

Courtney caught the gleam of moonlight on their guns and gave a moan of fear.

'Quiet!' Lefteris whispered fiercely, and clamped a hand over her mouth.

The thin Englishman was gesturing down to where they crouched among the trees and thick scrub. He shrugged. 'We'll never find them in that lot.'

Nikos swore. 'They can't have gone that far.' Standing at the edge of the road, his eyes searched the darkness for a betraying movement. Courtney's eyes were wide with fear above Lefteris's hand.

He was very still, his eyes narrowed as he watched Nikos prowl up and down before turning and relieving his frustration by emptying his gun into the tyre. Lefteris muttered an oath when he saw what was happening to his car, and his hand tightened on his gun.

'Why don't you shoot them?' Courtney whispered, wriggling free of his hand.

'And let them know exactly where we are? Don't be stupid!'

Three other men had arrived belatedly to join Nikos by the car and he snapped an order at them in Greek.

'What did he say?' Courtney asked nervously.

'Two of them are to go and wait at my house in case we go there, the third is to get some torches and reinforcements and follow us down this hill. He and Trevor, who must be that thin man, will make sure we don't get out by road.' The group by the crippled car were breaking up quickly. 'What's going on? No, don't tell me yet,' he said as she opened her mouth. 'We'd better get out of here first. Those men will be after us, and if they've got torches they'll be much quicker. Follow me, and be as quiet as you can.'

The first drop of the hill was very steep, and they slithered down between the trees until they came to more open scrub. It was rough underfoot, but at least

the bushes and the scattered rocks were big enough to
offer them some cover.

'We'd better head down to the river,' Lefteris said in
her ear and she followed him as he zigzagged between
the sage bushes and the clumps of holly oak. Stumbling
along behind him, Courtney envied him his swift
assurance. He had hardly hesitated, as if it were
perfectly normal to be shot at and chased down a
hillside. She had a terrible stitch in her side and longed
to rest, but the powerful torch beams swinging menac-
ingly above them were incentive enough to carry on.

She was gasping for breath when they reached the
river. There was a steep drop down on to the bed, but
she didn't even hesitate as she scrambled after him,
swinging round the slender trunks of the trees that
overhung the water and jumping off huge boulders.
Her one thought was not to lose sight of Lefteris. He
represented the only safety and sanity in this crazy
flight through the darkness.

'I can't believe this is happening to me,' she groaned
as he shot out a hand suddenly and dragged her behind
a clump of oleander.

'Shh!'

'What are you doing? she whispered urgently.
'They're right behind us!'

'Let's just see how far they're prepared to follow us,'
he whispered back. 'Now get down and keep quiet!'

They didn't have long to wait before they heard their
pursuers clattering over the stony riverbed. Their
voices echoed around the rocks and Courtney shivered.
They sounded far too close for comfort. She edged
closer to Lefteris's reassuring bulk.

'Can you hear what they're saying?' she breathed.

'Not really. Something about roads. One of them
seems to think they're wasting their time down here.
Let's hope the others believe him.'

He listened tensely, and after what seemed to
Courtney interminable minutes of discussion he

nodded. 'They're going back,' he said quietly. 'My guess is that they'll try and cut us off at the roads.'

They waited a few more minutes until the last sound of their pursuers had receded into the distance, then Lefteris beckoned Courtney out from behind the oleander. 'Stay very quiet, though,' he warned her. 'We don't want some bright spark deciding to come this way after all.'

The chase had kept her adrenalin pumping, but now that the immediate danger had passed Courtney found that she was shaking uncontrollably, and it took all her courage to follow him up the riverbank and up on to the hill beyond.

He was waiting for her at the top of the bank, half concealed in shadow. Reaching down a hand, he pulled her over the lip, frowning as he caught sight of her face in the moonlight. 'Are you all right?'

'Oh, fine!' she said acidly. 'I like a good chase in the darkness, especially when there are men with guns coming after me!'

Her voice was shrill, and she could feel hysteria bubbling up inside her until he took her firmly by the shoulders and shook her. 'Stop that!' he commanded. 'You can't go to pieces here!'

His strength seemed to flow through her. Courtney took a shuddering breath and nodded. 'Sorry,' she muttered.

'That's better,' he said, and dropped his hands. 'You'd better tell me exactly what's going on. Why is Nikos so anxious to get hold of you? I imagine it's not for your blue eyes!'

'No.' Courtney rubbed her face wearily. She told him what she had overheard as they set off across the hillside once more. 'I didn't know what they were talking about, but I was frightened, and when I tripped over that cat I just panicked and ran.' She paused and glanced up at him. 'I don't know what would have happened if you hadn't have come just then. I couldn't believe it was really you. The whole thing's just so fantastic. One minute I'm in the middle of a party, and the next we're running down the hill in the dark.'

Lefteris heard her out in grim silence. 'You didn't get any idea what it was they're going to so much trouble for?'

'Nikos just talked about "the stuff". I thought it might be drugs.'

'Something illegal, certainly. I understand why he's so keen to have you back. He doesn't want you running off to the police to tell them what you've heard. You know too many details for him to risk that.' He walked on in silence while he thought.

'What are we going to do?' Courtney asked humbly, after a while.

'We'll have to get to the police somehow.'

'We could phone them from Agios Giorgios,' she suggested eagerly.

'We can try, but if as much is at stake as there seems to be I wouldn't have thought Nikos's thugs will waste much time cutting the phone lines.'

Courtney was horrified. 'They can't do that!'

'We're not talking about peaceful, law-abiding citizens, Courtney,' Lefteris said with an edge of impatience. 'This isn't a game. If they're prepared to shoot at you—and I don't think they meant to miss— they won't think twice about cutting some phone lines.'

'Oh,' she said, deflated. 'Won't anyone at the party think of notifying the police?'

'Why should they?'

'They must have heard the shooting!'

'There's always shooting at parties. I don't suppose anyone gave it a thought. They'd all be too busy discussing how I'd come to take you away from Nikos.'

She glanced at him. Everything had happened so quickly that she hadn't had time to do more than take it for granted that he was there when she needed him, but now the full impact of his presence hit her. His

dark, forceful features, the reassuring solidity of his
body, the power and the control. . .he was *here*, close
enough to touch, and for a moment Courtney forgot
her fear and simply drank in the sight of him.

'How did you know where I was?' she asked after a
moment.

He didn't look at her. 'It wasn't difficult. Several
people saw you driving through the village with Nikos,
and he made very sure that everyone knew that yet
another English girl had fled from the wicked Markakis
family.' His voice was bitter. 'Nikos makes rather a
speciality of spreading rumours about how badly we
treat our women. He's been telling everyone you were
my fiancée.'

'What?'

'It makes a better story,' he said sardonically. 'Why
do you think everyone was invited tonight? They were
all there to see my woman living under his protection.
It was a matter of honour for me to come and fetch
you back,' he finished rather stiffly.

'I didn't know,' she said in a low voice. A matter of
honour? Was that all she had meant to him? 'I didn't
tell him that. . .that. . . I just told him I wanted to go
to Hania,' she said, desperate to convince him. 'He
passed me walking down the road and offered me a
lift. When he suggested I come here instead, there
wasn't much I could do about it. I didn't have anywhere
else to go.'

'You could have come back to me,' Lefteris said
tightly. 'You must have known I didn't mean all I said.'

They had stopped to face each other on the silent
hillside, and the memory of that last, bitter quarrel
hung heavily between them. Courtney could smell the
thyme drifting on the night air. Unable to look at him
properly, she stared down at a clump of sage by her
feet.

'I was too angry to think properly,' she said. 'And
then it was too late. I wished I hadn't gone with Nikos,

though.' Raising her eyes with difficulty, she faced him at last. 'I'm sorry,' she said simply. 'I should have listened to you when you told me not to trust Nikos. Now I've involved you in this mess.'

His expression was unreadable as he looked down at her, but she had the impression that he was relieved. Had he really thought she had gone with Nikos as a deliberate attempt to hurt him? 'It's just as well you have involved me,' he said after a moment. 'You're a girl who needs looking after.' Turning, he headed up the hillside before she could think of anything to say. 'Come on, we'd better keep moving.'

'Where are we going?' she asked, glad of the change of subject as she toiled after him.

'Agios Giorgios.'

Agios Giorgios!' she squeaked. 'But they'll be waiting for us there!'

'We're not going to walk up and introduce ourselves,' he said with a hint of asperity. 'We're going to get some food and some warm clothes.'

Courtney stared at him. 'Why can't we just borrow a car and drive down to Hania?'

'Because that's exactly what Nikos will expect us to try and do. He'll have every possible exit covered. There's no way he'll let us get through.'

'So we're stuck?' Courtney's fear came trickling back. 'There's only one way out of the valley.'

'No, there isn't.'

She looked at him in surprise. 'Is there another road?'

'We're not going to drive.' He stopped and pointed up at the mountains looming above them. 'We're going up there.'

Courtney gaped at him. 'To the mountains? *Why?* We won't find any police up there!'

'Of course we won't,' he said impatiently. 'But if we can get up to that ridge and then follow it round, we can get down to Xiloskalo.'

'Isn't that the place a the top of Samaria Gorge?'
'Precisely. First thing in the morning, it's full of buses dropping off people who are going to walk the gorge and heading back to Hania empty. It should be easy enough to get a lift.'

'But it'll take us days to get all the way over there!' Courtney objected, her heart failing at the thought of the climb. 'If we have to walk, wouldn't it be easier to walk over into the next valley?'

'It would be easier, but all these valleys have got just one road leading down to Hania. They're quiet too, and strangers are easily noticed. Xiloskalo is a much safer option, even if it is a long hike. But I can't take you all the way up there wearing that thin cotton dress. I'm going to ask Dimitra if she can give you something warmer.'

It didn't take all that long to reach the hillside above Dimitra's house, but it was hard going over the rough ground and Courtney was exhausted. She longed to stagger down to the village and fall into bed, but the unusual number of cars on the road below them reminded her of danger once more.

Lefteris pointed down at them significantly. 'What's the betting those are Nikos's men?' He pushed Courtney down behind a boulder. 'You stay here and rest. I'll go and see what I can find.'

'You will be careful?' In spite of herself, Courtney clutched at his hand like a frightened child.

Lefteris's smile gleamed briefly through the darkness. 'I will.' The sight of the cars patrolling the road below, looking for them, had chilled Courtney, but Lefteris didn't seem in the least bit scared. If anything, he seemed to be enjoying himself! 'Stay very quiet,' he instructed her. 'And whatever you do, don't move, or I'll never be able to find you again!' With a brief reassuring squeeze of her hand, he vanished into the shadows.

Courtney huddled behind her boulder, more grateful

than she cared to admit that all the decisions had been taken out of her hands. Lefteris would know what to do; she just had to do what she was told. She didn't like being left alone very much, but she was glad of the chance to rest. She had been warm enough when she was walking, but as the long minutes passed she got colder and colder, and she was soon shivering in her thin dress. In between the clouds, the moon was bright, and she began to worry. What if one of Nikos's men spotted Lefteris moving down the hill? What if they hurt him?

It seemed an eternity before he reappeared. He slipped through the shadows, avoiding the moonlight, so that he seemed to materialise out of nowhere. Courtney, aching with cold and exhaustion and fear, threw pride to the winds and clung to him. 'Are you all right?'

'Of course.' He put his arms round her and rubbed her briskly. 'You're frozen!' Shrugging a rucksack off his back, he pulled out a thick black dress. 'Dimitra's Sunday best! You'd better put it on over your dress. You'll be warmer that way.' He watched Courtney as she struggled into the dress and tugged it down over her own. She was much taller and slimmer than Dimitra, but fortunately the old lady wore her skirts long and it didn't look too ridiculous. Dimitra had sent her black kerchief too, and Courtney tied it over her hair, too glad of the warmth to worry about style. Ginny would have been horrified.

'You look like a real Greek widow,' Lefteris commented with a glint of humour.

She rubbed the small of her back and grimaced. She ached all over. 'I feel like one!' She nodded at the pack. 'How on earth does Dimitra come to have one of those?'

'Manolis — her son — is a mountain guide. This is his. He's away at the moment, so she's lent me one of his jumpers too.' He patted his chest, now covered in a thick, dark jumper that made him look more of a brigand than ever.

'What did she say when you crept up on her in the middle of the night?'

'She seemed to take it all in her stride. These mountain villages have always bred resistance fighters, and Dimitra's more than capable of facing down anyone who dares to ask if she's seen us. She's given us a blanket, a couple of bottles of water and what food she could throw together, so we should be able to make it to Xiloskalo without too much trouble.'

Below, the lights of Agios Giorgios beckoned invitingly. 'How long will it take?' Courtney asked with a sinking heart.

'It depends how far we get tonight. Fifteen hours, perhaps.'

She felt weak at the thought. 'I don't know that I'm cut out for this kind of trek,' she said nervously, as he packed everything away in the rucksack. 'Isn't there some other way?'

He gestured down to where two men were getting out of a car just outside the village. They held ominous shapes in their hands. 'You could always go and ask those nice men to give you a lift to the police,' he suggested.

Courtney watched the men walk stealthily along the road, their guns held rock-steady in their hands. 'Perhaps we'd better head for the mountains after all,' she said weakly, and Lefteris gave another of his swift, gleaming smiles.

'It won't be that bad,' he promised. 'And I'll be there to look after you.'

He would look after her. Courtney took a deep breath and straightened her spine. 'OK,' she said, and with a last, longing look at the comforting warmth of the lights she turned and followed his lean figure back up into the mountains.

* * *

She lost all track of time as they climbed up and up through the maquis in the dark. Her feet slipped on the rubbly stones underfoot, and she was scratched and sore where the thorn bushes caught at her bare legs, but she barely noticed after a while. Exhaustion deadened her senses and numbed her mind until she was conscious only of the effort involved in putting one foot in front of another.

She never knew how long it took them to reach a stone shepherd's hut built like an igloo high on the hills. Inside it was dark and smelt of goats, but there were a couple of wide stone benches covered in dirty straw.

'Not the most luxurious of accommodations,' Lefteris said with a wry glance around. 'But you need to rest. We'll stop here for a while.'

'Are we safe?' Courtney asked, lowering herself wearily on to the straw.

'For now.' He pulled out the blanket Dimitra had given him and spread it behind her. 'There isn't much point in them looking for us in the dark when they can wait until tomorrow and check the hills with a pair of binoculars. The slopes are so bare that it's easy to see anyone from a distance. That's why I wanted to get as far as possible tonight.' He glanced at Courtney, sitting numbly on the bench, and left the blanket abruptly to crouch before her to take off her shoes. For a moment, he held her sore feet, tightening his hands about them.

'Lefteris?'

'Yes?'

'What did you say to Nikos tonight?'

He looked up into her face with dark, implacable eyes. 'I said that if he came near you again I would kill him.'

Courtney swallowed, more than a little frightened by his expression, but the next instant he had smiled and it had gone. 'You're tired,' he said gently and released her feet. Lifting her legs on to the bench, he lay down beside her and settled himself as comfortably as he could on the straw before pulling her towards him and wrapping the blanket firmly around them both. 'There's only one blanket, so we'll have to keep each other warm.'

The solid strength of his body was inexpressibly comforting. Courtney rested her head on his chest and listened to the slow, steady beat of his heart. Through the open doorway of the hut, she could see the moonlight patterning the hillside in surreal white and black. It was a still, magical light which froze everything in timeless suspension, turning the scrubby bushes into crouching shapes that might at any moment resolve themselves into the mythical creatures of ancient Crete. Drifting into sleep, Courtney wondered why she didn't find the thought more frightening, and then remembered that she was safe in Lefteris's arms. I'll look after you, he had said. Nothing could hurt her now.

Manolis's jumper was tickly beneath her cheek. She sighed and snuggled closer to Lefteris's warmth, feeling the steady rise and fall of his chest. Was he asleep already? Suddenly it seemed very important that he know there was nothing between her and Gianni.

'Lefteris?' she breathed again.

'Mmm?'

'I'm not going to see Gianni in Rome. I never was.'

There was a pause, then his arms tightened imperceptibly about her. 'Good,' he said very quietly, and then, after a long silence, so long that she thought he had fallen asleep, 'Inger really is just a colleague.'

'She must be a very good colleague to bring you champagne during your siesta,' Courtney murmured, still jealous.

'Champagne?' He sounded puzzled. 'Oh, *that* time. . .how did you know about that?'

'I had to find the champagne for her.'

'She told me she'd helped herself,' he said grimly. 'I

told her to put it back where she'd found it. I won't have liars on my staff. It's just as well Inger is now looking for another job.'

She lay very still. 'She's leaving? But I thought she was supposed to be brilliant?

'She's certainly been good at her job, but she's not irreplaceable, and I don't take kindly to having my siestas disturbed—at least, not uninvited.'

Courtney smiled into Manolis's jumper. 'Oh,' she said, and asked no more, but when she fell asleep she was still smiling.

She wasn't smiling when he woke her a few hours later. There was a barely perceptible lightening behind the hills to the east, and she was stiff and cold and bad-tempered. 'Do we have to go already?'

'Nikos will send men up into the hills as soon as it's light.' Lefteris sounded brisk and horribly awake. 'It won't take them long to spot this hut. It's the only shelter there is around here, and if they've got a decent pair of binoculars they'll pick us up easily.'

'If you're trying to reassure me, you're not doing a very good job,' Courtney said grumpily. Her eyelids felt as if they were weighted down with lead and her muscles were cramped and painful. Any memories of last night had dissolved into the dark mists of sleep; she had a vague recollection of Lefteris taking off her shoes and looking fierce, but that was all.

Groaning, she manoeuvred her legs on to the beaten earth floor, and yelped as she tried to stand up. 'I can't walk!'

'You'll loosen up once you get moving again,' he said cheerfully.

She felt a little better after one of Dimitra's oranges, sweet and juicy and refreshing, and winced as she put on her shoes. She was convinced that she would be lucky to make it to the door, let alone to the mountain-tops, but Lefteris was annoyingly right. As her muscles

warmed up, the stiffness disappeared, and by the time
the dawn began to wash colour back into the landscape
she was amazed at how awake and invigorated she felt.

They followed narrow goat tracks through the
sparse, scratchy scrub. The soft prettiness of the olive
groves had been left far below them. This was a sterner
landscape: bleached rocky outcrops and stunted clumps
of thyme and thorn and thorny burnet with its prickly
halo. Only the tough could survive up here, Courtney
thought, her eyes on Lefteris's back. He looked utterly
at home in this bleak country, moving easily over the
rough ground.

'How do you know your way?' she asked when they
stopped at last for a rest. She sat down among the
thyme bushes to catch her breath while he leant against
a rock, relaxed but alert as he scanned the hill below
them for signs of pursuit.

'This is my home,' he said simply. 'You can't escape
from the mountains in Crete. Even by the sea, the
mountains are there, rising behind you. They are part
of what it is to be Cretan. We are a hard and stubborn
people, and the mountains have made us like that. We
have something of their wildness and their grandeur,
their cruelty and their pride.'

Hunkering down beside Courtney, he broke off a
twig of thyme and twirled it between his fingers, his
eyes on the soaring peaks. 'It's the mountains that have
helped us keep our identity. Crete was occupied for
hundreds of years, but we fought from the mountains
where no oppressor could follow. Whole bands of
freedom fighters lived up here during the Turkish
occupation. A man would marry, bring up a son, and
then disappear into the mountains to become a *palikari* — a brave one, a fighter — and in time his son would
do the same. The *palikaria* were renowned for their
bravery, and they were savage fighters, but they saw
themselves as heroes. Honour and gallantry were as
important to them as courage. They never gave up.'

He waved his arm at the desolate beauty of the hills spread out beyond and around them. 'This is perfect resistance country, riddled with caves and gorges. You can see how they could live up here for years and no one would ever find them.'

'Why are we worrying about Nikos following us, then?'

'Because we don't want to hide,' he said patiently. 'We want to get down to the police, and the quickest walking is through the most open country. They won't be able to catch us up here, though. It's just a question of getting down to the road again. We'll just have to hope Nikos doesn't think you're capable of walking all the way to Xiloskalo.'

'I don't know that I am,' Courtney sighed. 'We seem to have been walking for hours already, and it's only eight o'clock.'

He handed her the twig of thyme and she sniffed at it, crushing it between her fingers to savour its fragrance. 'Of course you are capable,' he said. 'You may not know it, but deep down you are a fighter, Courtney.'

'But I'm not! I've always been pathetic.'

'You're not being pathetic now, when it matters. You haven't cried and you haven't complained. You are being a true *palikari*, in fact! You've just kept going, and you'll keep on going until we get there. You don't need to fight a war to be brave. You just have to do something you thought you couldn't.'

Courtney was silent, thinking about what he had said, and imagining what it must have been like for the generations of men who had fought stubbornly for freedom. She didn't feel very brave. She would never have the courage to risk everything as the *palikaria* had done — at least, not unless Lefteris was there, too. It was easy to be brave with him.

He watched the thoughts chasing across her expressive face. 'Come on, *palikari mou*,' he said, getting to his feet at last and reaching down a hand to help her up. 'You haven't finished being brave yet. It's time to move on.'

CHAPTER NINE

For Courtney it was a day out of time. High above the tree line, the hills were bare except for the scattered maquis clinging stubbornly to the stony ground, and tiny alpines blossoming miraculously in their inhospitable environment. Courtney forgot all about Nikos as she stopped to exclaim over the exquisite star-shaped flowers, or to step carefully around a patch of purple aubrietia. After last night's frantic flight through the darkness, she felt utterly safe, cut off from the world below by the dazzling mountain air. The very thought of danger seemed unreal up here. There were no roads, no houses, no telegraph poles, not even a shepherd's hut to remind them that there was anyone else in the world at all. There was just the light and the flowers and the mountains — and Lefteris.

They stopped for lunch, perching above the scratchy maquis on a cluster of flat rocks to share the pies Dimitra had made into a packet for them. They were a little battered, but the pastry was still light and flaky, oozing with creamy cheese and fresh herbs. It was one of the best meals Courtney had ever had. At midday, the sun beat down on them, but the breeze was cool and sharp with the hot, dry scent of the hillsides. Far below them, the flat *tonk*, *tonk* of a goat's bell echoed up through the silence.

'That was heaven,' she sighed through her last mouthful of pastry.

He grinned at her contented expression. She had never seen him look so relaxed or so carefree, as if he too had forgotten why they were there. 'Why do I get the feeling that your deepest fantasies are reserved for food?' he teased.

Courtney picked a crumb of feta off her skirt and thought of the times she had lain awake and imagined his hands warm against her skin. 'Not always,' she said.

Glancing up, she saw that he was watching her and their eyes met across the bright air. Neither of them said anything, but he smiled, and after a moment she smiled back. To Courtney, it was as if a wordless conversation had taken place, and a tingling sense of happiness began deep inside, spreading slowly outwards until even her fingertips were quivering with it.

Then he turned away to inspect Dimitra's packet. 'There's one pie left,' he said quite naturally. 'Do you want to have it now, or keep it for later?'

'Now,' said Courtney promptly. She felt curiously exhilarated. High in the mountains, alone with Lefteris, only now mattered. She didn't want to look ahead, to plan for the future or what would happen when this long trek was over. For now, it was enough just to be with him. Besides, she was still hungry. There would be time enough to worry about later when later came.

He grinned and handed her the pie. Courtney broke it in two and handed half back to him. 'We'll share it,' she said.

Something flared at the back of his eyes as he took the piece from her. 'There was a time when I would never have expected an English girl to offer to share,' he said, looking up to the mountains still soaring above them. 'I don't think Sabrina knew what the word meant, and Linda certainly didn't. She wasn't prepared to share anything in that marriage.

He took a bite of his pie, remembering, while Courtney sat and watched him and wondered if she would ever be able to tell him how much she loved him. 'As soon as Linda arrived in Agios Giorgios she started trying to make Christos go back to England,' he went on after a while. 'Christos suggested that they spend half the year in England, half the year in Crete,

but that wasn't good enough for Linda. She loathed it
here. She was rude to my mother, quarrelled with my
sisters, and sneered openly at Agios Giorgios.' He
glanced at Courtney. 'Linda would never have bothered to talk to Dimitra, any more than she would have
thought to share a last pie.

'I never trusted Linda, but she was Christos's wife,
so we had to make the best of it. I thought it might
help if they had a house of their own, so I made them
a gift of Villa Athina, which had been standing empty
since my grandmother died. Linda was always complaining that I held the purse strings too tight, and the
house became legally theirs so that she would have no
grounds for complaint. I can't tell you how many times
I've regretted handing it over to that woman! Linda
thought Athina was too small, of course, and insisted
on having those extra rooms built on at the back, but
they never lived there. The marriage went downhill
very fast. Christos was miserable with her but too
proud to admit it, and Linda took to spending all her
time in Hania bars. That's where she met Nikos.'

His voice was very cold. 'Nikos saw a perfect opportunity to humiliate Christos, and the whole Markakis
family. There has always been enmity between our
families. No one knows when it began, or why, but
Nikos is determined to keep it alive. The Papadakis
family have an unsavoury reputation. Many of their
business ventures have failed, others have flourished
suspiciously, but they will never match the Markakis
wealth and prestige. Nikos knows that, and he hates it.
Humiliating us has become almost an obsession with
him, and Linda was an ideal tool. He can be very
charming when he tries, and he and Linda were soon
embarked on a very public affair. I don't know what
she wanted out of it. She was very vindictive, and I
think she knew that having an affair with Nikos of all
people would be doubly hurtful.'

He shrugged. 'We may have misjudged her. Perhaps

she was just bored, perhaps she wanted to provoke Christos into taking her back to England, but if so she miscalculated. When Christos realised what was happening, he had to accept that he had made a mistake. He told Linda that he was going to divorce her. That wasn't what she wanted at all. She didn't want to lose her hold on the Markakis millions. Quite suddenly she was all over Christos, playing at being a good little wife, but it was too late by then. He'd made up his mind. It wasn't an easy decision for him to make; divorce isn't as accepted here as it is in England.' Lefteris looked bleak. 'In the end, he didn't have to go through with it.'

'You said he was killed in a car crash?' said Courtney quietly, and he nodded.

'We'll never know for sure, but it may have been an accident. It was certainly a very convenient one for Linda. She thought she was going to inherit Christos's share of the fortune, and she was furious when she found out that most of it was tied up in the companies, and that she would only get an extremely generous settlement, as well as Villa Athina, of course. Frankly, we were glad to give her the money to get rid of her, and I offered her an extra sum to buy back Athina. She didn't want it, and we wanted to make sure that she was finally gone. Nikos obviously had a better idea. He suggested that she sell the villa to him. It would be a far sweeter revenge, he told her. She would get the extra money and have the extra satisfaction of knowing that we would hate what she had done.' Lefteris's face was very grim. 'Linda leapt at the idea. The villa has been a constant sore ever since, just as Nikos knew it would be. Every time I look at it, it reminds me of her and what she did to Christos. I'm surprised it took Nikos so long to think up the idea of inviting English tourists to stay there,' he added cynically. 'It must have seemed a perfect way to rub salt in the wound.'

Courtney stared down at a group of alpine crocuses

by her feet. They were very delicate with orange centres, bright and white and perfect. 'I thought you just didn't like English girls,' she said. 'I didn't realise that the villa was bound up with so many bad memories.'

'My mother died soon after Christos was killed,' Lefteris said. 'I think her heart was broken. She would never have been able to bear the thought of Nikos owning Athina. The rest of us just had to get on with life. Linda went back to England, my sisters married and when Nikos did nothing with the villa it seemed as if I could put everything behind me and concentrate on building on the company. And then you arrived.'

He paused and looked at Courtney, lit by bright sunlight. 'I thought that I was going to have to go through all that again. That first sight of you, standing half naked in the sunshine, convinced me that you were going to be as shameless as Linda or Sabrina. They were both very fond of flaunting their undoubtedly beautiful bodies. I was fully prepared to despise you in the same way, and when you fell over yourself to be charming to Nikos that first morning that only seemed to prove that you were just like them. But then I began to wonder. . . I saw how hard you worked to clean that house, and everyone in the village kept telling me how nice you were. I used to see you sometimes, walking through the trees with your arms full of bread, or sitting on the terrace smiling at the sun.' He hesitated. 'Whenever I met you, you were impossibly prickly and I'd tell myself that you were just as bad as all the rest, but somehow, in spite of myself, I found myself liking you. I didn't even know why. I think it was probably because you seemed to be so happy in Crete.'

'I was,' said Courtney. He liked her! It might not be love, but for now it was enough. She lay back, stretched out her arms to feel the warm rock beneath her hands and wriggling her shoulders to make herself more comfortable. Glancing up, she found him watching her and smiled. 'I am.'

The breeze had tangled her hair into dishevelled streaks of gold, and her face was still glowing from the climb. In the diamond-clear light, her eyes reflected the deep blue of the mountain sky, and the corners of her mouth tilted upwards. Relaxed on the rock, slender legs drawn up and face turned up to the sun, she was almost unrecognisable as the wary girl who had arrived in Crete less than a month ago.

She still wore Dimitra's Sunday best. It hadn't taken her long to warm up once they started walking, but Lefteris had refused to let her take off the black dress, which was hot and uncomfortable over her own dress. 'Black passes unnoticed on the hills,' he had said, 'but that pink dress will stand out a mile. If you're going to take anything off, it had better be that.' Courtney had grumbled, but obeyed. She had been glad enough of the warmth last night, but she was sweltering now under the thick black cotton. The long sleeves were rolled up to her elbows, and she had unbuttoned the front as far as she dared to let the cool breeze at her throat.

Lying now on the rock, she closed her eyes with a contented sigh and hitched the skirt up to cool her bent knees. A welcome gust of breeze ruffled the skirt against her thighs and she smiled lazily.

Lefteris caught his breath, and her eyes jerked open. 'What is it?'

His smile was rather twisted. 'I think it would be a great mistake for you to immerse yourself in the past, *glykia mou*, when you have just learnt how to appreciate the present. Are you still determined to study the Minoans?'

A jet was crossing the blue high above them, its vapour trail curving away into nothingness. Courtney stared up at it. 'I suppose so,' she said. She didn't want to think about what she would do. Lefteris might have accepted that she was nothing like Linda, but he hadn't said anything about staying, had he? His face was etched in startling clarity against the sky behind his head and she thought, irrelevantly, I'll never forget this moment. No matter what happens, I'll always be able to remember him like this. No, she wouldn't think about the future now.

'What does *glykia mou* mean?' she asked to change the subject.

'It's just an expression,' he said, but his eyes flickered. 'It means "my sweet one".'

Faint colour tinged her cheeks. Don't take it seriously. He'd said it was just an expression. that's all it was. 'I thought I looked like an old widow?' she reminded him, trying to keep her voice light.

'That was last night,' he said. 'You don't look like an old woman now, Courtney. Far from it.' He lifted a strand of sun-bleached hair. 'You were quiet and brown when you arrived, but the Cretan sun has turned you to gold.'

Courtney was finding it hard to breathe. He's going to kiss me, she thought. Please let him kiss me! *Please*.

But he didn't kiss her. Instead he reached out and drew the black cotton slowly back over her knees, his hand sliding tantalisingly along her smooth thigh. 'This is no time for sunbathing,' he said wryly. 'Or anything else. You're far too relaxed for a girl being chased across the mountains by men with guns!'

'Nikos.' Courtney sat up, sobered suddenly as she too remembered their danger. 'You don't think they'll have given up?' she asked hopefully. 'We haven't seen any sign of them and there's no reason why he shouldn't just cancel the arrangement for the landing of whatever it is, and bluff it out. After all, it would only be my word against his, and he could make up some innocent explanation for what I overheard.'

'He'd be hard pushed to find an innocent explanation for shooting at us,' said Lefteris. 'I don't think Nikos would have pursued us that far if there hadn't been some reason why he couldn't cancel the operation. The whole deal will be at risk if he can't stop us getting to the police before tomorrow night. I'm sure they'll be concentrating on stopping us getting down off the mountains. We can't do any harm up here, and they may well have spotted which way we're heading.' He got to his feet, hoisted the pack on to his back and picked up the shotgun. 'That's a risk we've got to take.'

Once the thought of Nikos had intruded into her idyll, Courtney found it hard to push it away. The magic of the day had dimmed and she grew increasingly tired as they climbed on and up. She wished she hadn't noticed the gun again. It had been easy to ignore before, but now it kept catching the edge of her eye, an uncomfortable reminder that they hadn't outrun the danger. It was still there, waiting for them.

They reached the snow in the early evening. Courtney remembered how she had first seen the snow-capped mountains and marvelled at how impossibly remote they had seemed. And now here she was, touching the snow. Close to, it lost its ethereal white-ness and was disappointingly dirty where the dust had blown. It lay in patches, tired after the winter, and melting drip by drip even as she watched.

She had never been so high. They were right among the tops of the lower range of mountains, their peaks rounded and weathered, and the sage bushes limp and brown where the snow had lain heavily upon them. The higher peaks still rose above them, but to Courtney's relief the long climb was over. Instead they scrambled on to a rough track that wound along the ridge, following the gradient between the rounded peaks. It was their first sign of civilisation all day.

'The shepherds use this in the summer,' Lefteris explained. 'It's easy walking now. All we have to do is follow this to Kallergi.'

'Kallergi?'

'It's a mountain refuge run by Austrians. Climbers and walkers use it as a base for exploring the White Mountains, so we should be able to spend the night there. It overlooks Samaria Gorge, which means we'll have an easy walk down to Xiloskalo tomorrow morning.'

'You mean we don't have to sleep in another hut like last night?' Courtney asked, brightening.

'I hope not. With any luck, we should get a bed, a wash *and* some food.'

The prospect put new bounce into Courtney's step. After the scramble uphill, walking along the track was blissfully easy, and at first she swung along beside him, but it wasn't long before she began to despair of ever getting there. It seemed as if they had been walking forever; the track kept twisting away round the hills, and it was getting late before they finally spotted the refuge perched on an outcrop of slanting rock, with the stark, sheer face of Mount Gigilos looming behind it.

The refuge was a neat, modern building with a dramatic view down into the Samaria Gorge, but Courtney was too tired to care by the time she got there. It might be the most spectacular gorge in Europe, but all she wanted was to sit down. The lights were on in the hut and from inside came the sound of cheerful voices. A wiry man came out to meet them in the entrance hall, which was lined with professional-looking walking boots set neatly on wooden shelves. Lefteris drew him aside and explained their situation in a low voice, while Courtney took off her shoes and sat staring blankly down at her bare feet, too tired to do anything but let him take care of everything. After a while, the man nodded briskly and went inside.

'Franz is going to try and get me through to the police on their radio,' said Lefteris, pulling Courtney to her feet. 'You can have a shower while I'm doing that, and then he'll find us something to eat.'

Courtney stood under the shower and vowed she

would never take plumbing for granted again. It was
bliss to let the water stream through her hair and wash
off the dirt of the last two days, and when she had
finished she felt immeasurably better, if still light-
headed with exhaustion. She found Lefteris in the
dining area, sitting at one of the tables and looking, as
ever, peculiarly at home. The room was full of people
dressed in sensible walking gear, and Courtney hesitated in the doorway, very conscious of her bare feet,
her shapeless widow's outfit, and the hair hanging
damply to her shoulders.

Lefteris waved her over and introduced her to the
Austrians who ran the refuge. There had been too
much static to get through to Hania, he said, but they
would try again in the morning. Courtney nodded, too
weary to worry much about Nikos now. She let Lefteris
do all the talking as she devoured a bowl of hot soup
and a huge plate of pasta, vaguely conscious of the
conversation around her in several different languages.

She felt detached from it all. The room was warm
and cheerful, and she was safe and clean and well fed.
She tried to concentrate on the table but the plates
kept swimming out of focus, and she would blink and
jerk herself upright, only to find her head drooping
forward again almost immediately. Beside her, Lefteris
was deep in conversation, and, succumbing to temptation at last, she let her head fall against the broad
strength of his shoulder.

'I think she's tired,' someone said in amusement.

'I think she is.' Lefteris's voice seemed to come from
a long way away. Courtney tried to force herself to sit
up and pretend to be awake, but her eyelids wouldn't
obey her. 'Have you got anywhere we can sleep? It
looks as if you're busy tonight.'

'All we can spare is a mattress,' said one of the
voices. 'Do you mind sharing?'

Courtney surfaced momentarily to find herself lifted
in strong arms and carried up some steps. She tried to

mumble something about being able to walk, but
Lefteris ignored her. She was laid down on a plain
mattress, and a blanket tucked around her. Courtney's
eyes wavered open with a huge effort to find him
leaning over her.

'You will come too?' she murmured, scarcely aware
of what she was saying. 'You won't leave me alone?'

'I'm coming later, *agapi mou*,' he said quietly. 'Sleep
now.'

Reassured, Courtney abandoned herself to the sleep
lapping at the edges of her mind. She had no idea what
time it was when he eventually came back. She stirred,
mumbling an incoherent protest as he shifted her over
to one side of the mattress to lie down beside her.
Conscious only that his warmth represented comfort
and security, she rolled back towards him, sliding her
arm over his body and snuggling against his lean
strength. He had taken Manolis's jumper off, and his
shirt was soft against her cheek. Dimly, she was aware
of him muttering something beneath his breath as his
arms folded tight around her, but it meant nothing as
she pressed her lips to his throat with a contented sigh
and sank back into sleep.

It took just over an hour to get down to Xiloskalo from
Kallergi. Most of the buses arrived at about eight
o'clock so they set off just before seven. After the
previous day's dawn start, Courtney felt as if she had
been allowed a lie-in, and her heart was light as they
crunched across a patch of snow down to the track. She
was clean and rested, breakfast had been substantial,
and a light breeze just lifted the hair away from her
face as she walked down beside Lefteris. The mountain
air was exhilaratingly clear and she could feel the sun
on her back.

They had no more success with the radio, but Franz
had promised to keep on trying until they got to the
police themselves. In a few hours, it might all be over.

Courtney had a strange end-of-holiday sensation, a determination to make the most of the time she had. Her fear of Nikos had receded overnight; in the bright morning light, the whole idea of danger seemed absurd.

Her confidence lasted only as long as it took them to walk down the winding track above the Omalos plateau. A narrow road cut straight across the flat plain, and they could see tiny buses and cars moving along like matchbox toys, all heading for the cluster of buildings that marked the top of Samaria Gorge. They were above the car park when Lefteris's hand shot out and jerked Courtney to a halt.

'What's the matter?'

'Look down there.' Her eyes followed his pointing finger with a chill sense of foreboding. The car park was crowded with buses and cars and groups of walkers checking they had everything they needed before embarking on the long walk down the gorge to the Libyan sea. In the middle of them all, gleaming and somehow sinister, was a red Mercedes that was all too familiar.

'Nikos!'

'They must have spotted us heading up to Kallergi,' said Lefteris grimly. 'After that I suppose it would be obvious we would come this way. Whatever else he is, Nikos isn't a fool, and he obviously wants you very badly indeed.'

'It's nice to be so popular!' Courtney tried to make a joke of it, but her voice was unsteady, and Lefteris took her hands, holding them tightly between his own.

'Don't look like that, *palikari mou*. We're not beaten yet.'

'But we can't stay in the mountains forever!' Courtney clung to his hands, fighting down panic. The sight of the red Mercedes had shaken her back to ominous reality.

'We're not going to.' His cool, calm voice was infinitely reassuring. 'Remember, we've got Franz as a

back-up. He agreed that if he hadn't got through by
midday he would go down to the police himself, just in
case we hadn't reached them. All we need to do is
keep out of Nikos's way for a few more hours.'

'But he's obviously expecting us. Once everyone's
gone down the gorge, he's bound to see us if we try to
slip past.

'Not if we go down the gorge too,' He let go of her
hands with a final comforting squeeze. 'I know you're
tired of walking, but there's safety in numbers. He
won't be expecting us to head on down the gorge, and
with any luck he won't notice us in the crowd.'

'But what about the police?'

'We'll have to rely on Franz. Now, listen.' He
pointed down into the car park once more. 'See that
big group standing around the information board down
there?' Courtney nodded. 'We should be able to slip
down behind them without Nikos seeing us. I'll go and
get the entrance tickets and leave a message for Franz
telling him what's happened, if you go and get some
food in the shop. It's a long walk down and we'll need
something to eat.'

'What if Nikos sees me?' she asked, panicking at the
thought of being on her own.

'He won't see you if you're careful. He's looking for
a girl in pink, remember, and there are masses of
people going in and out of the shop. It shouldn't be too
difficult to hide behind them.'

Courtney swallowed. She was more frightened than
she had been since Nikos first snapped at the thin man
to follow her. 'It's all right for you,' she muttered. 'But
I'm just not cut out to be a heroine!'

'Come on, you've been a true *palikari* so far,' said
Lefteris encouragingly. 'You can't give up on me now!'

He helped her down the last steep bit of the path,
and pulled her into the middle of a group of Germans
who were listening to a guide giving instructions about
the walk through the gorge. Ignoring their disapproving

looks, Lefteris turned Courtney to face the information board as if they were intent only on the walk before them.

'You know what you've got to do?' he asked in a low voice, handing her some money.

Courtney was sure that there was a flashing arrow over their heads pointing them out to Nikos. She stared fixedly at a notice declaring that the EC had officially proclaimed Samaria Gorge to be one of the most beautiful areas in Europe — category A — just in case there had been any argument about it. 'I — I think so. Just go to the shop and buy some food. What could be easier?'

'There are water points along the way, so don't worry about drink. I'll try and persuade the guy in the ticket office to get a message to Franz as soon as possible, and I'll wait for you around here. OK?' Courtney nodded dumbly, and Lefteris's finger flicked her cheek. 'Try to act naturally, *koritsi mou*. Be as quick as you can, but whatever you do, don't run. Anything out of the ordinary will just attract his attention.'

Courtney took a deep breath. 'All right. I'm ready.'

'Good girl.' He patted her on the back, and she began to edge towards the back of the crowd, nearly collapsing with fright when she caught sight of Nikos, standing watching the milling crowds with hard eyes. Strangely enough, once the first shock was past, she felt better for having seen him. At least she knew where the danger was. Keeping her head down, she shuffled behind a group of Italians who were all talking animatedly as they headed for the shop.

The shop clearly catered for walkers, for there were piles of filled rolls and an array of snacks, as well as drinks and postcards and brochures. Courtney seized four rolls and a couple of bars of chocolate, and hoped the boy behind the counter wouldn't notice how much her hands were shaking as she fumbled for the money.

Two young men with enormous rucksacks were just getting ready to leave, and she slipped out with them, making sure to keep their bodies between her and Nikos. Her heart was pounding and the adrenalin roared in her ears so loudly that she was certain Nikos would hear it. Where was Lefteris? Her frantic eyes were so busy searching the crowds around the notice board that she didn't at first realise that the two men had veered off to join some friends, taking their protective shield of rucksacks with them. Courtney froze. The milling crowds seemed to have vanished, leaving her utterly alone and exposed in the middle of the car park.

Suddenly she spotted Lefteris, talking to a couple and looking for all the world as if he was part of a jolly group. The sight of him was enough to snap Courtney into action and she hurried towards him, only to stumble in her haste and sprawl on to the ground, still clutching her bag of rolls. Her involuntary exclamation made people turn to see what had happened, and the two young men began to move back towards her to see if she was all right. Over by the shop, Nikos turned to see what the commotion was about.

Lefteris got to her first. 'Courtney! Are you all right?' he asked urgently, his face taut with fear.

She nodded shakily and he pulled her to her feet, glancing over his shoulder. 'Has he seen us?'

'I'm afraid so,' he said, but gave her no time to panic. 'Come on, we'll have to hurry.' He held her tightly by the hand, and dragged her through the group queuing to show their tickets at the entrance to the path. Ignoring the muttered complaints of the British about people who didn't know how to queue, he waved his tickets above their heads at the kiosk and together they plunged down into the gorge.

CHAPTER TEN

THE path into Samaria Gorge dropped over three thousand feet in just two kilometres before it reached the riverbed. The original *xiloskalo* — wooden steps — used by shepherds to climb up out of the gorge had been replaced by a zigzagging path with wooden handrails, but it was still a dizzyingly steep descent and Courtney's knees were soon trembling with the strain. Her feet skidded on the loose, gravelly stones and tripped over the tree roots as Lefteris dragged her down, down, down into the gorge.

She had no time to appreciate the pine trees shading the path, or the blue haze of the mountains stretching into the distance ahead. She had no time to stop like everyone else and crane her neck back to stare up at Gigilos looming above them, the sun shining sharp and clear on its bleak face. For Courtney, it was all a blur of trees and rocks, a seemingly endless skid around hairpin beds, and a confused impression of overtaking straggling groups of walkers who all stared disapprovingly at their haste. Afterwards, she remembered only the sharp, dry scent of the pines, the firm grip of Lefteris's hand around hers and the sound of water, faint but unmistakable, far below.

At last they reached the river itself, tumbling busily along between massive, weather-worn boulders and over rounded stones. Plane trees hung over the water, dappling the rocks with green sunlight. Lefteris let her rest there, hidden out of sight of the path by a boulder carried down by the winter torrent and beached between two trees.

For a long time, Courtney could only lean against the rock, whooping and gasping for breath, but after a while she had recovered enough to kneel by the river. She splashed cold water over her hot face and bathed the gravel from the grazes on her knees and palms where she had fallen. It was cool and quiet in the green shade of the planes, and there was something very soothing about the murmur and chuckle of the water over the stones.

Sitting back on her heels, she flicked the water from her hands. Shimmering drops still clung to her eyelashes and trickled down the front of Dimitra's dress as Lefteris helped her to her feet. He turned up her hands so that he could inspect the grazes on her palms.

'Do they hurt?'

Courtney looked down at his fingers holding hers. Every detail of his hands seemed preternaturally clear as he rubbed his thumbs very gently over the grazes. 'Not really,' she said huskily. 'It was my own fault for panicking. If I'd kept my head, Nikos might not have noticed me at all.'

'I saw you come out of the shop,' Lefteris said in a voice that she hardly recognised. 'One minute you were safe behind those trekkers, and the next you were lying on the ground.' He paused. 'I thought. . .I was afraid he had shot you.' Quite suddenly, he put his arms round her and held her tightly against him. 'Don't do that to me again,' he said into her hair.

Unable to speak, Courtney shook her head into his shoulder, and he dropped his arms as abruptly as he had seized her. 'We'd better keep moving,' he said, stepping back to pick up the rucksack.

'Do you think Nikos will really follow us?' she asked, amazed at how calm her own voice sounded, but she couldn't look at him. Her body burned with awareness of him, her senses sang where he had held her, but his air of normality confused her.

'He'll follow us all right,' he was saying as he shrugged on the pack once more. 'I'd guess that he won't be in too much of a hurry, though. Now that we're in here, he knows that we can't get out except by going down to Agia Roumeli with everyone else, and there's only one way out of Agia Roumeli, by boat. All he has to do is contact some of his stooges and get them to watch the ferries.'

'So we're trapped down here?'

'Hardly.' He gestured around at the towering scenery. 'It's a pity Nikos saw us, but this is a big place. The boy at the ticket office promised he'd get a message up to Franz, so we'll just have to trust him to contact the police. In the meantime, we've got to make Nikos think we're in a hurry to get to Agia Roumeli, and lose him later on.'

'Why don't we lose him now?' she suggested. 'He won't see us if we hide here until he's passed.'

'No, but he'll ask people further down if they've seen us. As soon as he suspects we're not ahead of him any more, he'll start retracing his steps.'

'Oh.' Courtney sighed. It made sense. 'I feel as if we've been running for weeks,' she said as he helped her back down on to the path. 'At least it's keeping me fit!'

Walking was much easier now that they had reached the river, and although Lefteris still kept up a brisk pace she didn't have to run to keep up any more. It gave her a chance to look about her as they followed the riverbed. It was easy to see why the gorge was only open in the summer: in winter a great torrent of water must crash down between the mountains, carrying trees and great boulders with it. The water was quiet now, scarcely more than a stream, spilling over the stones into glacial blue pools or disappearing underground for a while, only to re-emerge in a swirling pool just when she had forgotten that it had ever been there at all.

Pine needles lay along the path as it climbed up from the river to where tiny cyclamen grew wild in the shade, and then led back down to the river again. After the barren Cretan mountain-tops, Courtney felt as if

she had tumbled into a different country altogether.
The trees grew thickly up the steep sides of the gorge,
the dull, dark colour of the pines contrasting with the
fresh lime-green of the planes that clustered by the
water. Sunlight slanted through the leaves or burst into
a clearing, dazzling them after the cool shade. Above
them, the mountains soared, their massive silence in
sharp contrast to the constant burbling of the water,
and so high that Courtney got a shock every time she
looked up, as if they had loomed up without warning.
Afterwards, her memories were all of contrasts: light
and shade, sound and silence, the rocks and the water
and the green, green trees. And of Lefteris, moving
ahead of her along the narrow path with that loose,
easy-jointed walk of his, or turning to help her across
the stepping-stones as they crossed and recrossed the
river.

Where the gorge bent round towards the Libyan sea,
the valley widened and the trees ended abruptly. The
path took them along the dry riverbed, between
tumbled, sun-bleached boulders. Away from the pines,
Courtney could smell the more familiar scent of the
mountains, the unmistakable fragrance of thyme and
the drift of sage on the air. The climate was different
down here, for the thyme bushes were about to burst
into flower and the sage was decorated with delicate
pink spires. Courtney touched them gently with her
fingers, wishing she could linger. She hated Nikos for
making her rush past all this beauty.

Lefteris let her rest again when they reached the
ruined village of Samaria. Deserted when the gorge
was declared a national park, the cluster of houses
were slowly crumbling. Some still had their roofs, but
the wooden stairs had long rotted and the rooms were
used only by goats now. Others were open to the sky;
wild flowers flourished on in the doorways, and fig
trees grew wild by fireplaces.

At midday, the village was far from deserted. Marking the halfway point of the walk, it was a popular place to stop for lunch, and there were tourists sitting at wooden tables under the trees, or in the shade of the ruined houses, exclaiming at the wonders of the gorge in a babel of different languages. Courtney and Lefteris sat in a patch of meadow under an old olive tree. Clover grew so thickly that the ground was a haze of white, blurred with poppies and wild geraniums, and the air was sweet and still. Fat bumble bees blundered among the flowers, and sparrows hovered hopefully for crumbs as they ate their rolls.

'It's so peaceful here,' Courtney sighed, leaning back against the tree. 'I wish we could just forget about Nikos and stay here.'

'We will,' promised Lefteris. 'But not until we've persuaded him that we're really on our way to Agia Roumeli.' He stood up, brushing the crumbs off his trousers for the sparrow. 'He should be here soon. We want to be ahead of him, but not so far ahead that he can't see us for himself, so get ready to move quickly.'

Barely five minutes later, Courtney clutched at his arm as they watched the walkers crossing the sturdy wooden bridge to the village. 'Here he comes!' They were well hidden behind a crumbling wall, but even so she shrank back. Nikos was hesitating on the other side of the bridge, evidently unable to decide whether to go on or not. He looked hot and angry, and the sight of him brought a chill draught of menace to this idyllic place.

He's coming to check the village,' Lefteris said with satisfaction. 'As soon as he starts poking around the houses, we'll get back to the path.'

Courtney was sure that people would start pointing at the surreptitious way they kept peering round the wall, but nobody, it seemed, was interested in anything but their lunch packs. Nikos had reached the village, his eyes scanning the crowds in an ominously professional way as he began a stealthy tour of the

buildings. As soon as he was out of sight, Lefteris and
Courtney ducked back over the bridge.

'Don't go too fast,' said Lefteris, pulling her to a halt
once they were safely over on the other side. 'We want
him to see us.'

'You may want him to see us,' she muttered. 'I don't.
What if he shoots us?'

'He won't do anything with all these people around.
Anyway, it looks as if he hasn't got much more than a
pistol with him, and that won't be accurate at this
distance.'

'Oh, just a pistol!' Courtney said ironically. 'Why am
I worrying, then?'

He grinned. 'Trust me! Now, pretend you've got
something in your shoe, will you? I want to see what
he's doing.'

Obediently, Courtney stooped to shake out one of
her moccasins while he glanced over her bent figure.
'He's seen us!' he said, and jerked her upright. 'Let's
get going! We don't want him to catch us now.'

They practically ran along the path, pushing past
walkers who evidently felt that they weren't taking the
gorge in the right spirit. The mountains were closing in
again, squeezing the river between sheer, soaring rock
walls, until there was virtually no room to pass. They
had to keep crossing the water to find a dry bit of path,
and Courtney's feet were soon wet.

Stumbling over the stones, she hardly registered the
grandeur of the landscape, but not even the thought of
Nikos close behind them could detract from the sheer
drama of the narrowest point of all. Barely an armspan
in width, the walls of the ravine towered a breathtaking
two thousand feet above, as if they had been rushing
towards each other only to stop at the last second
before the crash.

'Portes,' said Lefteris, seeing her awed gaze travelling up and up and up to the narrow strip of sky. 'The
Iron Gates. It's quite a sight, isn't it?'

The river was so narrow that only one person could cross at a time, and it had caused a bottleneck among the walkers. The overwhelming size of the gorge had absorbed the crowds up to now, and Courtney was taken aback suddenly to see so many people gathered together all at once. Reluctant to leave the highlight of the trek behind, they stood around, laughing as people wobbled across the submerged stepping-stones and making sure that if anyone fell in it would be recorded for posterity on video.

Somehow, Lefteris managed to drag Courtney through the waiting crowd towards the stones. The river flowed much faster between its rock walls, and they had no choice but to cross one set of stones to a little bouldery beach, then back to the other side before edging carefully along the smooth rock until a final set of stepping-stones led back to the path.

Lefteris was behind Courtney, and she turned to watch him jump sure-footedly across. To her astonishment, he suddenly lurched sideways and fell up to his knees in the bitterly cold water, much to the amusement of those watching from the safety of the stony beach.

'What on earth did you do that for?' she asked as she helped him out. 'That water's freezing!'

'I wanted to make sure that we'll be remembered in case Nikos stops to ask if we've been this way. Quick, let's get out of sight. He won't be far behind us.'

Once they had negotiated the stepping-stones, most people turned round to watch the fun, and no one noticed as Lefteris pulled Courtney behind a vast boulder that was sheltered from the path by a burst of pink oleander.

They didn't have long to wait before Nikos appeared. Courtney was disappointed to see that he managed to keep his feet dry as he pushed through the cheerful crowd, and she cowered behind Lefteris's comforting bulk when he stopped almost in front of the boulder where they hid. He looked about him carefully, then asked a man with a video camera something. Courtney saw the man nod, and point on down the path, and a satisfied grin flickered across Lefteris's face as Nikos strode on with renewed determination.

'He'll be sure we're on our way to Agia Roumeli now.' He helped Courtney out from behind the boulder. A couple passing gave them a surprised look of disapproval, clearly wondering what on earth they had been doing hidden in the bushes, but Lefteris merely gave them a bland smile. 'All we have to do now is make our way back to Samaria. There's usually a warden there with a radio, so we can try and get through to the police again, just to check whether Franz got through with the message.'

But when they got back to the village, the warden's house was locked. '*Ade!*' Lefteris banged on the door in frustration. 'He must have gone to Agia Roumeli for some reason. Well, we'll just have to make the best of it.'

'It was all right for Goldilocks,' grumbled Courtney, trying to peer through the windows. She was tired and crotchety after the long walk back up the gorge. 'She could just walk into any old cottage she found in the woods and help herself to porridge and a bed. We haven't got anything to eat or anywhere to sleep.'

'Stop complaining,' said Lefteris in an infuriatingly good-humoured way. Courtney could hardly recognise the harsh, unsmiling man who had discovered her by the roadside. This Lefteris was relaxed, utterly at home in the wild mountains and far, far more attractive than he had ever been before. 'We've got a blanket on the ground,' he said. 'What more do you want?'

Desire battling with exhaustion left Courtney feeling twitchy and with a sharp edge to her voice. 'A hot bath would do for a start, followed by some clean clothes, a new pair of feet and a good, square meal!' She watched him spreading the blanket out on the soft clover and sighed. 'Do you think we'll ever sleep in a bed again?' she asked, hearing the unthinking intimacy implied in her question too late.

He looked up, and his dark eyes gleamed with amusement when he saw her blushing. 'I hope so,' was all he said, but something in his voice made her heart lurch uncomfortably aginst her ribs.

'I — er — I think I'll go and wash,' she said hurriedly.

The last of the walkers had long departed, and she was quite alone. Lefteris was somewhere out of sight. Courtney stripped off Dimitra's dress and stood thigh-deep in the river, letting the river run cool against her hot skin, remembering the look in his eyes. Ducking her head under the water to rinse her hair, she gasped at the cold, and tingled with freshness as she rinsed out her underclothes and left them to dry in the last of the sun. With a mental vow never to wear black again, she pulled on Dimitra's dress once more and made her way back to the blanket.

She sat cross-legged on it while Lefteris went to wash, combing the tangles out of her hair with her fingers. When he returned, wearing only his trousers, his thick black hair was damp and slicked to his head and his skin had a sheen of health and vigour. Courtney had to wrench her eyes away from his bare chest as he threw himself down on the blanket beside her.

'That feels better,' he said. His dark eyes were bright and held the lurking smile that always made her pulse thump slow and insistent.

She nodded, pretending to be absorbed in disentangling her hair, but beneath her lashes she could see the muscles flexing beneath his skin, and her fingers trembled with the desire to reach out and touch him. She wished she knew how he felt. Was he teasing, simply trying to distract her, or was that smile really for her?

'What are you thinking about, *glykia mou*?' His voice was like a caress, and Courtney shivered as if he had stroked her.

'When you came to take me away from Nikos,' she said hesitantly, not looking at him, 'was it really just a matter of honour, as you said?'

He never took his eyes from her averted face. 'You know it wasn't,' he said softly.

'Then why did you come?'

'Because I missed you.'

Courtney's fumbling hands stilled and dropped from her hair as she turned her head to look at him at last, hardly daring to believe what she was hearing.

'When you walked out on me, I was furious,' he said in the same deep, steady voice. 'I told myself I was well rid of you, that you were just like Sabrina and Linda, but I knew that you weren't. I think I've known ever since I first kissed you. That night we came back from Hania, you were like fire in my arms. I wanted to catch you up and spend the rest of my life making love to you, and if there had been any way I could have stopped my guests arriving the next day I would have done. That's why I didn't think it was very sensible to have kissed you, though I can't say I had any regrets. As it was, I just had to try and keep my hands off you for the week. It wasn't easy, seeing you every day and remembering how you had kissed me and not daring to touch you in case I lost control altogether.'

He reached across and took her hands, turning them up so that he could kiss each palm where it was grazed from her fall. 'I spent the whole week wild with frustration because you seemed to have withdrawn and were intent on being nice to everyone except me — especially Gianni.'

'I thought you were having an affair with Inger,' Courtney confessed, her fingers curling around his like bindweed. 'She was like Ginny, beautiful and clever and glamorous. . .and she wasn't English.'

'Inger is all those things,' he agreed, 'but she has never had a hold on my heart. I've always thought of our relationship as being a purely business one, but this time she was cloying, always there when I wanted to be alone, drawing me aside for intimate little chats when I wanted to watch you. She guessed how I felt about you. She must have seen the way I looked every time you came into the room and decided that if she was ever going to marry the Markakis organisation—which is what she really wanted—she would have to make an effort. It didn't do her much good. All I could think about was you and Gianni. I was so jealous and angry, I couldn't think properly.'

'Is that why you were in such a rage when you came back from the airport?'

'I was a fool,' he admitted. 'I thought you were really planning to go off and join Gianni and I just lost my head. I said some unforgivable things to you that night, but after you walked out it only took half an hour for me to realise quite how stupid I'd been. I came after you, hoping you'd be with Dimitra, but you'd gone. They told me they'd seen you driving past with Nikos.' His fingers tightened around hers. 'I was devastated! I wondered if I might have been wrong about you after all, that you might have turned out to be another Linda, but I realised that it didn't matter. I had to have you back. I came to take you back from Nikos as publicly as possible so that everyone would know that you were mine.'

Courtney could feel happiness beating at her heart, so intense that it was almost scary. Her eyes shone in the golden light, and she smiled as she reached out for his hands. It was wonderful to know that she didn't have to pretend any more. 'You got more than you bargained for,' she said, thinking of that terrifying chase through the night.

'I did,' he grinned. 'But you were worth it. You were so lovely up on the mountains, it took all my self-control to keep my hands off you, and I had to keep reminding myself that the most important thing was to keep you safe. I thought it would be better to wait until this was all over, but you didn't make it any easier for me. Last night, you rolled into my arms and kissed me, just here.' He touched the pulse that beat just below his ear. 'If you hadn't been dead to the world. . .! You didn't even know what you were doing.'

Courtney smiled, a slow, slow smile, and leant forward to press her lips against his throat once more, right where his jaw met his ear. His skin smelt clean and warm and masculine. 'I know what I'm doing now,' she whispered.

His eyes blazed with desire as he returned her smile and pulled her down with him on to the blanket. 'We've got all evening and all night,' he said, his voice very deep and warm with promise. 'It's a long time until we can have something to eat, I'm afraid. Are you hungry?'

'Ye-es,' she said cautiously, confused by the abrupt change of subject.

'Me too. We'll have to distract each other.'

He ran his hand up the smooth length of her thigh, and Courtney quivered beneath his touch.

'What did you have in mind?' she asked huskily.

'A Greek lesson.'

'Oh.' Courtney couldn't keep the disappointment from her voice, and Lefteris smiled again. Propped up on one elbow, he slid his hand beneath her hair and spread it out, letting it fall between his fingers with a soft shimmer.

'Dimitra hasn't taught you the words you really need,' he said, and she swallowed.

He was hardly touching her, but she was throbbing with the hazy excitement of his body so close to hers, and her eyes were dark and wide with desire. 'What words are those?'

'We'll start with the most important one.' He leant closer. 'Put your arms around my neck and repeat after me: *s'agapo*.'

Courtney's hands trembled as she lifted them to his

shouders, unable to stop them moving over their sleek strength. 'What does it mean?' she whispered.

'It means "I love you",' he said, looking into her eyes. His voice was very deep and warm. 'Aren't you going to repeat it? You'll never learn Greek unless you try.'

'*S'agapo*,' she said, letting her arms slide further around his neck.

He pretended to tut, but his eyes were dark and smiling. 'You haven't got the pronunciation quite right. Say it again, this time with more feeling.'

She smiled. '*S'agapo*.' Her fingers tightened against his skin. '*S'agapo*.'

'That's much better.' He was tantalisingly close, his mouth almost touching hers. 'We'll soon have you word perfect,' he murmured, and then the teasing was over as his lips claimed hers.

Courtney had no thought of resistance. Her arms pulled him closer and she abandoned herself utterly to the piercing sweetness of their kisses, to the spiralling excitement of his hands on her body and the demand of his mouth. They were both breathless and smiling when Lefteris lifted his head. He held her head between his hands and looked down into her face with such warmth in his eyes that Courtney wondered if this could really be the same fierce man who had found her on that dusty mountain road.

'I love you,' he said softly. 'Tell me that you mean it.'

Courtney's hands stretched luxuriously over his bare back, feeling the muscles flex between her fingers. 'I mean it,' she said, her eyes very blue. 'Of course I mean it.' She pulled his head down to hers. '*S'agapo*,' she murmured against his lips, and he was smiling as he kissed her again.

'Courtney. . .*glykia mou*. . .' His mouth drifted down her throat, his fingers were at the buttons of the black dress, sliding it off her shoulders, over her hips, down the slender length of her legs until she arched in uninhibited pleasure at the touch of his hands on her nakedness. 'Are you still hungry?' he teased breathlessly, his hands sliding warm and possessive over her curves.

She shook her head, adrift on a sea of electrifying sensation, conscious only of his mouth and his hands and his lean, powerful body.

'Not at all?' His lips drifted to her breast and she quivered with need.

'Only for you,' she gasped. 'Only you.'

She could feel him smiling against her skin. 'Good,' he said, and bent his mouth to hers once more.

The sun hadn't yet reached the bottom of the gorge when they set off the next morning, but Courtney was impervious to the chill. She was intoxicated, still glowing with the joy Lefteris had shown her as the evening had faded into darkness, and the darkness into dawn. The first walkers were only just setting off from Xiloskalo, so they had the gorge to themselves. They didn't talk very much as they walked back down to the Iron Gates, but every time Lefteris touched her Courtney felt as if she would dissolve with happiness.

She was alive, invigorated, her senses so attuned that she could feel the earth turning beneath her feet. The mountains themselves seemed to have woken with her joy, their great seams of rock thrusting up towards the sky, pushing against each other at sharp angles or submissive curves. Pink-spired sage bushes clung to the cliffs, and, far above them, an eagle circled slowly.

Courtney got her feet wet again as she crossed the river at the Iron Gates, but she laughed as Lefteris pulled her off the last stepping-stone and into his arms.

'*S'agapo*,' she murmured into his ear, and he held her tight and kissed her.

'I think you're nearly ready to move on to lesson two!'

'Very touching,' a voice sneered behind them, and they jerked apart with shock. Nikos stood blocking the path, and in his hand he held a gun. Despairingly, Courtney realised that Lefteris's gun was strapped to the back of his pack. They had been so happy, so confident this morning that it had seemed impossible that they would ever need it.

'I knew what must have happened as soon as my men told me you hadn't got on any of the ferries,' Nikos was saying in a conversational tone that sat eerily with the unwavering gun. 'It was too late to come back then, so I left Agia Roumeli nice and early this morning. As you can no doubt imagine, I was anxious to catch you on your own.' His smile made Courtney's blood run cold. 'You've caused me a lot of trouble, Courtney Shelbourne. A *lot* of trouble. One of the most lucrative operations I've ever set up has been ruined by your eavesdropping. My best men have been arrested, and the entire cargo has been impounded. You must be very pleased with yourselves.'

'Your cargo must have been very valuable for you to go to all this trouble to stop us,' Lefteris commented. Courtney marvelled that he could sound so cool. 'What was it?'

'Drugs,' said Nikos curtly. 'Did you miss that while you were creeping around my house, Courtney?'

'I gathered it was something immoral,' she said shakily, taking an instinctive step closer to Lefteris.

There was cold anger in Nikos's eyes. 'It's easy for you to talk about immorality, isn't it? You've found yourself a much better meal ticket, haven't you?' He jerked his head at Lefteris. 'A few million here or there is nothing to your lover here. I don't blame you for putting yourself on a plate for him, but some of us have to work for a living.'

'Dealing in drugs isn't work,' said Lefteris contemptuously, and added something softly in Greek that

tightened Nikos's finger on the trigger and pinched his
nostrils white.

'Come over here,' he snarled. 'I want to see the look
in your eyes when you die.'

Courtney's mind was utterly cold and clear, still
shocked by the abrupt switch from happiness to horror.
She took a tentative step forwards, as if mesmerised by
the gun.

'Come on!' he said savagely.

Courtney wasn't looking at Lefteris, but she could
almost feel him tense. She took another step, stumbling
against the smooth stones and fell with a cry of alarm.
It didn't distract Nikos for more than a second, but it
was enough for Lefteris to go for him in a murderous
dive that took them both crashing on to the path.

Courtney heard the gun go off, ricocheting off the
rocks with a terrible noise that echoed horribly between
the towering walls of the gorge. She scrambled up,
terrified that Lefteris had been shot, but he was grap-
pling with Nikos as they rolled on the ground, gasping
and grunting. As she watched, the heels of her hands
pressed to her mouth in horror, Lefteris managed to
force Nikos's arm back until the gun fell from his
fingers with a clatter on the stones, skittering down to
lie wedged between two boulders.

The noise seemed to revitalise Nikos. With a mighty
heave, he pushed Lefteris off and tried to reach for the
gun, but Lefteris recovered quickly and leapt on him
once more. Courtney, snapping out of her petrified
trance, stumbled over to where the gun lay, and
scrabbled frantically between the stones with fingers
that seemed thick and unwieldy. She managed to get
hold of it at last, but her hands were shaking so much,
she nearly dropped it again.

It was heavier than she had expected, and she had to
hold it with both hands. She stared helplessly down at
it, forcing herself to take a firmer grip. All she had to

do was point and shoot, surely? It always looked easy on television.

The gun shook in her hands as she pointed it uncertainly down at the two men struggling on the ground and tried to shout stop, but all that came out was a croak, and they either didn't hear or ignored her. This was no clean fight for squeamish television audiences, and Courtney shuddered. Nothing in her suburban English upbringing had prepared her for the raw savagery in the air, or the men fighting at her feet with a pitiless ferocity that seemed part of the very landscape.

She didn't dare shoot in case she hit Lefteris. She could only stare down at them, fear choking her throat. As if in slow motion, she saw Lefteris draw back a bunched fist, and then Nikos's head jerked back and lay limply against the stones. Suddenly everything happened at once. A group of uniformed men came running along the path, erupting into the narrow area just as Lefteris got slowly to his feet and stood looking down at his bloody hands.

The air was full of shouted questions and excited exclamations, but he ignored the policemen. Courtney was still standing with the gun in her hands and tears streaming down her cheeks, but as Lefteris hesitated a few feet away the gun dropped from her nerveless fingers and she took a step towards him at last. The next moment, she was in his arms, and he was holding her so tightly that she could hardly breathe. Courtney clung to his massive, reassuring strength as desperately, caring only that he was alive and whole.

Later, she sat on a rock, wiping her face with unsteady hands while an animated discussion in rapid Greek swirled round her. After much explanation and consultation, two policemen helped a groggy Nikos to his feet and bore him off, his hands firmly secured behind his back. One who was clearly an officer lingered for a final word with Lefteris, and then he too was gone, leaving them alone at last.

Lefteris crouched by the river to wash the dust from his face, and rinse the blood from his hands. Then he came to sit beside her on her rock and linked his fingers tightly with hers. They said nothing for a while, content to sit alone and let the stillness and silence soothe them while the water hurried past, clear and cool and impervious to mere human dramas.

'How did the police know we were here?' Courtney asked at last.

'Franz got our message through just as he promised, and thanks to his information the police were able to pick up almost everyone last night. It was quite a haul for them. According to Michalis, the officer in charge, it'll make international headlines, so they're happy. They didn't have anything on Nikos, though — just your word against his, and he was careful not to appear at the drop just in case. Apparently they've had their suspicions about him before now, so this time they decided to keep him under surveillance. As soon as he started up the gorge, they followed him, but not too close in case he got suspicious. They hadn't heard any more from us since Franz's message, so they assumed we were down here somewhere. They heard the shot when I tackled Nikos, and began to run, but they were so careful about keeping their distance that it was all over before they got here.'

'*Is* it all over?' Courtney asked, hardly daring to believe it.

'It's over as far as Nikos is concerned.' Lefteris turned her face up to his. 'As far as you and I are concerned, we're just at the beginning,' he said, and he kissed her.

Afterwards, Courtney only remembered snatches of the journey home: the Libyan sea rolling against the harsh hillsides in bright turquoise waves, sitting among the nets on the little fishing boat that took them to

Hora Sfakion, the nerve-racking road up to Imbros and on down to the north coast once more, arriving back at the villa and the sweet welcome of the orange trees.

That afternoon, she stood on the terrace beside Lefteris and looked up at the mountains. Already the long trek up to the snow line seemed remote, unreal, as if part of a dream. Dimitra's dress had been laid aside for the last time, and she was clean and comfortable in the same silky dress she had worn to Hania. With a contented sigh, she leant against Lefteris.

His arm came round her. 'Time we started on lesson two,' he said with a smile.

'Don't you think I need more practice on lesson one?' said Courtney, remembering how last night's joy had begun.

'Lesson two is very easy.' He turned her to face him. '*Tha me pandreftis*?'

'That's not easy,' she pretended to complain.

'It is for you. It means "will you marry me"?' Lefteris's smile was warm as he held her hands. 'All you have to do is remember the Greek for yes — but be careful! You know how easily you muddle up yes and no!'

Courtney smiled but pulled away from him slightly to look up at him seriously. 'I thought you didn't think marriage was worth the price?'

'Not unless I was absolutely sure I'd found the right woman, I said,' he reminded her. His hands tightened on hers. 'And I *am* sure.'

'I'm too. . .too ordinary for you,' she burst out, suddenly assailed by doubts. He was so rich, so successful. What if he got bored with her? 'You need a smart, sophisticated wife who can make clever conversation and entertain your guests.' Someone like Ginny, she thought despairingly, but Lefteris only smiled.

'No, I don't. I need you.' He put his arms around her and pulled her close. 'I don't want a sophisticated wife. I want a girl who talks to goats and takes care never to tread on flowers. I want a girl who needs looking after, and I'm used to looking after you now. You're everything I need. I'm not going to give you up now.' His hands tightened against her. 'Say you'll marry me, Courtney,' he said in a voice that was suddenly fierce and urgent with desperation, and her eyes shone blue and clear as she looked up at him and took a deep breath.

'*Ne*,' she said and he laughed with relief.

'At least you got it right when it mattered!'

'I hope you don't regret it,' she warned him, half joking, half serious, and he turned her face up to his.

'I won't,' he said. 'And if you ever do, I'll just take you back up to the mountains and remind you what it was like when all we had was each other. No luxuries, none of the comforts you'll be used to by then. Just the essentials, you and me and a blanket on the ground.'

Courtney relaxed into him, slipping her arms around his back and remembering with a shiver of pure happiness how they had explored the limits of joy together. 'I won't mind,' she smiled into his throat. 'Sleeping on the ground last night wasn't so bad!'

'Tonight will be even better,' he promised. 'We'll be warm and clean and have a soft bed to share.'

'We don't have to wait until tonight, do we?' she murmured.

Lefteris drew her closer. 'No, we don't have to wait.'

Welcome to Europe

CRETE — 'land of legend'

Crete is by far the biggest Greek island, so it should be no surprise that it has something for absolutely everyone. It's a great place for a holiday whether you're interested in walking, nature, art and archaeology, lively nightlife, watersports — or simply relaxing on superb beaches! For the young — or the young at heart! — there are the busy resorts of the north-east coast with their discos and English pubs, but if peace and quiet is what you're after the south coast is the place for you. The sheer variety Crete has to offer is a reflection of thousands of years of intriguing — and often tragic — history.

THE ROMANTIC PAST

Crete was the cradle of European civilisation — so it seems appropriate that it was known in legend as the birthplace of **Zeus**, ruler of the gods. The story tells that **Cronis**, who at one time was the supreme god, so feared that one of his children would overthrow him that he ate all the babies his wife **Rhea** gave birth to! But when Zeus was born, in secret, in a cave, his mother hid him and gave his father a stone wrapped in

swaddling clothes to eat instead, so that the baby was
able to grow up. . .and overthrow his father as had
been prophesied.

Later in life Crete was where Zeus, disguised as a bull,
brought the princess **Europa**, who became his lover
and mother of his sons — one of whom was the legendary **King Minos**. And, according to Cretans, Zeus is
buried here: the outline of his helmeted head can still
be seen in Mount Youktas!

Since the earliest times Cretan history has been a tale
of violence and resistance: the island has been con-
quered innumerable times. The Cretans have always
been known for their fierce independence and amazing
heroism — they have never ceased to struggle against
invaders, often at enormous cost to themselves. One of
the most famous examples of this occurred in 1866, at
the monastery of **Arkhadi**, high up in the mountains.
Cretan fighters, as well as their women and children,
were using the monastery as a refuge and the Turks
laid seige to it; when it became clear that there would
be no escape, the defenders blew themselves — and
thousands of their enemies — sky-high rather than sur-
render. The occasion is still commemorated every year
on its anniversary.

THE ROMANTIC PRESENT — pastimes for lovers. . .

Every visitor to Crete should be sure to see the palace
of **Knossos**, famous as the home of the legendary King
Minos — and of his wife's illegitimate monster child,
the **Minotaur**. . .half-man, half-bull, devourer of young
men and maidens. When excavations began at Knossos
in 1900, it soon became clear that the myths had at
least some basis in fact: the archaeologist Arthur Evans
uncovered the remains of an enormous and wealthy

palace, the centre of the first European civilisation; a civilisation which worshipped nature and valued the arts of peace. . .perhaps the basis for the legend of **Atlantis**.

The palace has been partially reconstructed, so that you can walk through rooms that are much as they were three thousand years ago, decorated with copies of the original stunning **frescos**. You can see the remains of Europe's first flush toilet, in the Queen's apartments, and still in place are the enormous storage jars, in one of which King Minos's young son is supposed to have drowned in honey. . . Knossos is almost always busy, but you can usually find a quiet corner in which it's easy to imagine that you've stepped back a few thousand years. . .

Most visitors to Knossos will pass through the city of **Heraklion**—so called because it was the site of the seventh labour of Hercules, which was the capture of the terrifying Cretan Bull, father of the Minotaur—and it would be a pity not to linger. Heraklion may be a busy, noisy, very modern place, but it's certainly worth a visit. Of course there's the **Archaeological Museum**—one of the most important museums in the world—where the treasures from Knossos and other Minoan sites are displayed; you'll be able to see the original frescos, as well as beautiful jewellery, pottery and many other artefacts. After a thorough tour of the museum you'll be glad of a rest and perhaps a tempting sticky pastry and a coffee in the museum's charming little open-air café, looking out over the city.

But there's more to Heraklion than the museum. The ancient **harbour** is certainly worth a visit, with its impressive **Venetian castle** which is open to the public. For a unique view of the city you can climb up to the city walls, where you'll find the grave of Crete's and

Greece's most famous modern author, **Nikos Kazantzakis**, who is especially well known as the writer of *Zorba the Greek*.

While you're in Heraklion you mustn't miss the **market**, which is one of the best you'll find anywhere, particularly for all kinds of food and spices. Even if you're not in the mood to buy — and there are surely few who could resist the array of souvenirs of all kinds — the loaded, colourful stalls and lively atmosphere will linger in your mind.

If you can manage to spend an evening in Heraklion, you'll be able to take part in the *Volta* — the traditional evening stroll, especially around Liberty Square and its beautiful public gardens. Why not take a seat at a café and watch the world go by?

Away from Heraklion and the other modern towns and resorts of Crete, life goes on much as it always has. If you are lucky enough to visit one of the villages, you may see a traditional wedding in one of the ancient Greek Orthodox churches. In the past Cretan brides would have **three crowns** placed on their pillows: a crown of thorns to symbolise long life and endurance of its trials; a crown of myrtle and orange leaves to symbolise sweetness and lifelong love; and a crown made of bread to symbolise peace and plenty.

Weddings are still celebrated with **music and dancing** — dancing was supposedly invented in Crete! The traditional Cretain instrument is the **lyre**.

Food is delicious all over the island, but the Iraklion area has some particular delicacies of its own: watch out for *stiffado*, beef cooked with onions and spices, and *giouvarlakia* — meatballs served with rice and a delicious sauce. At Easter a special soup, *mageiritsa*, is served. It's made from lamb's liver, vegetables, rice and egg.

No meal is complete when you're on holiday without at least a glass of local **wine**, and Cretan wine is excellent, both red—**Brousko**, **Kissamos** or **Minos**—and white: **Gortinos** and **Phaestos**. For something rather stronger, why not try the famous **raki**, which is a powerful spirit made with the skins and stalks of grapes? But be careful. . .! If you're feeling more abstemious—or suffering the effects of last night!—perhaps you should try some Cretan **herb tea**. The most famous variety is made from the herb **dittany**, which only grows on the island, and should certainly do you good: wild goats, it's claimed, ate it when they were wounded and were then rejuvenated and able to escape from hunters!

Crete is a shopper's paradise! If you've been to Knossos you may well be tempted by a piece of **pottery** with a design copied from one of the Minoan frescos—or there are plenty of other more modern designs. Near **Malia**, in particular, there are many large pottery factories with shops which offer a huge choice. But save some of your money—you may also want to buy textiles, particularly **embroidery**, or **carved wood**, **jewellery** and **shoes**.

DID YOU KNOW THAT. . .?

* Crete only became part of independent united Greece in **1913**.

* Crete is the birthplace of the famous artist **El Greco**.

* Cretans traditionally were firm believers in **vampires**.

* The Greek currency is the **drachma**.

* The Greek for 'I love you' is '*s'agapo*'.